SAY CHEESE

MARY BLAKESLEE

Cover by Jay Leach

Scholastic-TAB Publications Ltd.

Scholastic-TAB Publications Ltd.
123 Newkirk Road, Richmond Hill, Ontario, Canada L4C 3G5

Scholastic Inc.
730 Broadway, New York, NY 10003, USA

Ashton Scholastic Limited
165 Marua Road, Panmure, PO Box 12328, Auckland 6, New
Zealand

Ashton Scholastic Pty Limited
PO Box 579, Gosford, NSW 2250, Australia

Scholastic Publications Ltd.
Holly Walk, Leamington Spa, Warwickshire CV32 4LS,
England

Canadian Cataloguing in Publication Data
Blakeslee, Mary
    Say cheese

ISBN 0-590-73176-9

I. Title.

PS8553.L34S39 1989   jC813'.54   C88-095029-3
PZ7.B58Sa 1989

9 8 7 6 5 4 3 2 1   Printed in Canada   9/8 0 1 2 3 4 5/9
Manufactured by Webcom Limited

For Norma Mooradian

Chapter 1

My name is Granny Tyler.

Now, wait. Before you start imagining a little grey-haired lady with sensible shoes and a cookie aroma, let me explain. My full name is actually Granada, as in that part of Spain where my parents spent their honeymoon and where I got started. I'm an ordinary fifteen-year-old girl with dark red hair and sneakers.

The only thing really different about me is that one Saturday last September I found myself debating whether falling from a tall building or swallowing an indigestible foreign object was the easiest way to go. I really couldn't see any other alternative, since I can't stand the sight of blood (especially my own) and there was absolutely no way I could continue going to school at Fineacres High after what had happened that afternoon.

It had all started the Thursday before when Maureen and I were deciding which clubs to join. All the different organizations set up booths on the second day of school so that freshmen and transfers could see what the school had to offer in the way of extra-curricular activities. Maureen was a freshman here last year, but this is my first year at Fi High. In fact, it's my first year at any public high school.

You see, I've been in Switzerland at a girls' boarding school ever since Mom died when I was seven. Everything I know about North American public education would fit on the end of a pin. So I was very grateful when, soon after I arrived in Canada, I met this friendly kid, Maureen Chase, who took me under her wing.

Maureen already knew what she would be doing after school, of course. She'd joined the drama club last year and intended to spend every possible waking moment this year emoting. But I was a different matter; I hadn't a clue. So Maureen spent Thursday afternoon leading me around from stand to stand while I checked out what each had to offer.

I'm pretty athletic, so I'd already decided to sign up for basketball tryouts. Now I needed something less physical to round out my free time. Music and art aren't my thing and I'm not good at games like bridge or chess, so I was having a little trouble choosing something when I saw this incredible looking guy standing behind the school newspaper booth.

"Wowsers! Who is that?" I whispered to Maureen, gesturing to where the blond god was talking to a startling looking brunette flanked by two rather faded copies.

"Who? Oh, you mean Steve Williams. He's the editor of the *Fi High Speaker*. Gorgeous, isn't he?"

"Golly, he's incredible. How can I meet him?"

"First, you've simply got to stop saying 'wowsers' and 'golly.' Also 'shucks' and 'swell.' This is the eighties, you know. And second, the best way to meet Steve would probably be to sign up for a job on the paper. But it won't do you much good. He's Lonnie Kaye Borgnine's personal property."

"Who's she?"

"That's her over there talking to him now. The one with the overstuffed pink sweater."

The startling looking brunette — I might have known. However, I'm not one to turn down a challenge. I grabbed Maureen by the arm and marched determinedly across the grass to the newspaper booth.

"Hi. I'd like to sign up for the paper, please," I announced brightly as I edged in front of the other three girls. I gave Steve my very best smile too, hoping fervently that the sun hadn't brought out a new crop of freckles while I wasn't looking.

He turned from the other girls and smiled back. "Sure, you can sign up," he told me, "but I'm afraid that doesn't guarantee you a spot. You'll have to submit a sample of your work first, then we'll decide whether we can use you or not. Are you a writer?"

3

"Ah . . . not exactly." The fact is that English is about my worst subject.

"Art? Maybe you'd like to work on layouts."

This was much worse than I'd expected. "No, art really isn't my area."

He was beginning to look a little exasperated, and the three girls were starting to giggle behind my back.

"I guess you must be a photographer then. That's not such good news; we already have a guy who does all our camera work. But you're welcome to drop off some of your stuff anyway. I'll look it over, and if it's really good we'll give you a try."

"I — I'm not so sure . . . " But he had already dismissed me and turned back to the girls.

Maureen pulled me away before I could make a fool of myself. "I've got to hand it to you, Granny, you sure don't care who you take on. Lonnie and her groupies will be out to get you for that little manoeuvre."

"What are you talking about? He was open for business, wasn't he?"

"Yeah, but not the kind of business *you* had in mind. So now what are you going to do?"

This whole social thing was foreign to me. There seemed to be all sorts of rules I knew nothing about, having spent the better part of my life practically in a nunnery. What was wrong with letting a boy know you liked him, anyway?

"I'm going to submit samples of my work, of course. Then he'll hire me and I'll see him every day, and pretty soon we'll start dating."

"You really have been isolated from the real world, haven't you?" She sighed and shook her head. "Well, if you're determined to go for it, we'd better get those photographs of yours and give them to Steve today. Maybe, if you're really good, you'll get lucky."

"There's just one problem," I said as we headed for the bike stand. "I haven't got any photographs."

She stopped dead and stared at me. "But you told Steve…"

"No, he told me."

"Oh, Granny! You're hopeless." She grinned and took my arm. "Let's get something fattening over at Andy's and forget this whole silly business."

"But I can't do that. How am I going to get Steve to notice me if I'm not on the paper? And besides," I continued after a moment, "I do have photographs."

"But you just said —"

"They're not mine. They're Father's."

She dropped my arm and turned to face me. "Granny, you can't submit your father's work. He's a professional photographer. Steve would know his stuff isn't yours. Besides, it's dishonest."

"You're right, it is dishonest, but it won't

hurt anything. As soon as I'm taken on the staff of the paper, I'll be doing all my own work. No one will ever know."

Before she could protest any further, I jumped on my bike. "Come on, we'd better hurry before he closes shop." And I started peddling furiously up the street.

Fortunately, Judy and the twins weren't home when Maureen and I got there, so I didn't have to think up any explanations for what I was about to do. Judy, I should explain, is Father's new wife. They got married six months ago and moved to Vancouver, which is why I was finally released from my almost-cloister in Europe and brought back to Canada to live like a normal teenager. The twins, Trixie and Trina, are Judy's by a previous marriage. They're five years old and so cute you just want to squeeze them — until you get to know them better. Judy's consuming passion in life is to get them launched as child models, which, in my nastier moments, I think is why she married Father in the first place. He's fifteen years older than she is and balding, but he *is* one of the top photojournalists in the entire country.

"Follow me," I told Maureen as we dropped our bikes on the lawn. "Father's studio is at the back of the house." I led the way to a small windowless building at the rear of the property, then felt along the top of the door jam till I located the key. I slipped it into the door, knowing that with Father away on an assignment in South America it would be safe to go in.

I'd been in the darkroom only a couple of times since I moved in five weeks ago, but I was pretty sure I knew where Father kept all his rejects. Maureen followed me as I went to the back of the room and started ploughing through a tall filing cabinet.

"I really don't think you should be doing this, Granny," she whispered.

"It's all right, you can talk in a normal voice. Nobody's around," I told her. Other than that I ignored her as I pulled out a file folder labelled *Toronto Zoo* and started riffling through it.

"Just perfect," I muttered, selecting half a dozen of what I thought were the best shots. "These should do the trick." I slipped the pictures into a brown envelope, turned off the light, and opened the door.

"Are you coming back with me?" I asked Maureen.

"Well, I certainly can't leave you to do it on your own."

Steve was gathering up his stuff ready to leave when we got back to the school. Lonnie Kaye and her buddies were nowhere in sight, which I felt was a positive sign.

"Here are a few samples of my work," I lied, laying the envelope on the table between us. "I hope you like them."

His glance as he raised his head was puzzled. Then a light seemed to dawn and he smiled that amazing smile. "Ah, yes, the photographer. Let's see what you do." He picked up the envelope and slipped the photos out. I continued to smile while Maureen held her breath beside me.

After a day or two he looked up. "These are really quite remarkable, ah . . . what did you say your name was?"

"Granada. Granada Tyler."

"Yes. Well, Granada Tyler, we'll give you a try. Stop in at the office tomorrow after your orientation classes. It's in the basement in the family studies area, right beside the home ec kitchen. I'll give you your first assignment then."

"Assignment?"

"Sure. Might as well see how you make out right away. The first edition comes out next Tuesday, so you'll have to have your stuff in by Monday. That'll give you the weekend to shoot." He picked up the big box he'd been loading his stuff into and dazzled me again with his smile. "Well, so long. I'll see you tomorrow."

I stared after him, unable to move. Maureen grabbed me by the arm and shook me. "Boy, you've really done it now. All you have to do is come up with a bunch of winning shots for the assignment he gives you. Do you suppose your dad has any good pictures of the kids at Fi High?"

I ignored her sarcasm and smiled tolerantly at her. "No problem. I'll just borrow one of Father's cameras and shoot whatever he wants me to shoot."

"Don't you have your own camera?" When I didn't answer, her eyes opened wide. "You're not telling me you've never used a camera, are you, Granny?"

"Well, sort of. But I've watched my father work. It can't be that hard. As far as I can tell, you just point and press the button."

If only it had been that easy.

Chapter 2

"What I'd like is a bunch of candid shots of the football team. They'll be practising tomorrow afternoon, so you can get them then. The majorette corps should be working out about the same time. I want you to be sure to get lots of shots of them too."

As he finished speaking, Steve handed me a sheet of paper with a bunch of lines and boxes on it.

"Be sure to fill this in with the shot number and the subject. We have to be sure we get the right caption under the right photo." He grinned and added, "Good luck, not that you need it. From the look of your samples, you're already a pro."

I took the sheet from him and grinned back. It was all turning out as planned. I'd spent most of the evening before and all day in class thinking about how I would act toward Steve when I met him after school. I wasn't sure whether I should be strong and forceful like Julie Romano or more sweet and dumb like Mallory Keaton. I finally decided on the strong and forceful type, since it seemed to be more like the real me.

"A piece of cake," I answered confidently. As I turned to leave the room, I heard a voice call out from a desk at the back.

"I saw your photos; they're really good. What kind of camera do you use?"

I looked over to where the voice was coming from and saw a rusty-haired skinny guy looking up at me.

"Camera? I . . . ah . . . I use various kinds. It depends on what I'm shooting." I reached for the door, anxious to get away from any more questions, when Steve's voice stopped me.

"Wait a minute, Granada. You'd better meet your rival. This is Gary O'Hare, ace photographer and sometime drummer. Gary, this is Granada Tyler. She's new to the school."

The redhead got up and sauntered over. "Nice to meet you. Are you from another school here in the city?"

"No, I've been at a boarding school in Switzerland." I tried once again to escape, but as I moved toward the door the way was blocked by Lonnie Kaye Borgnine.

"Oh, my!" she smiled unconvincingly. "Boarding school in Switzerland, eh? You must find us *colonials* pretty small time."

Steve looked embarrassed and Gary scowled.

"Not really," I answered in my best Loni Anderson voice. "It was quite an ordinary school, and rather dull. I'm very glad to be here now."

"I'll just bet you are." She gave me a quick up and down look, then turned her back to me. "Steve, are you about ready to leave? We were supposed to meet the gang at Andy's twenty minutes ago."

"Lonnie, I'd like you to —" I didn't wait for Steve to finish the introduction, just slipped past her and out the door. Behind me I could hear Steve's voice muttering, "You didn't have to be so rude. She's just a kid."

"Just a kid, eh? We'll soon see about that," I announced to the startled janitor who was pushing a broom ahead of me. Maureen was right. Lonnie and I obviously weren't destined to be bosom buddies.

Maureen had drama club Friday nights, so I walked home alone. I'd met a few kids since school started, but I wasn't on snacking terms with any of them yet. It would probably be better for me to go straight home anyway. I could use the time to familiarize myself with one of Father's cameras before I had to use it the next day.

Judy and the twins were out again when I got home. But I did find a note on the kitchen table: *Be back soon. Put the casserole in the oven at 5:30 if we're still gone. Judy. P.S. Your father has been delayed and won't be back till tomorrow evening.*

That was *not* the news I needed to hear. I had planned on having him give me a crash course before I had to take the photos on Saturday. I took a look at his cameras the night before, after Steve said he would be giving me an assignment, and discovered that it was a little more complicated than just pointing and shooting. There were dials with numbers and parts that rotated and all sorts of weird things to push.

Oh, well, I decided, I'd just have to figure it out myself.

After a futile half hour, I realized I would have to find some sort of instruction book. The whole thing was quite beyond me. I searched through the stack of books on Father's desk until I finally found what seemed to be the manual that fitted the Nikon FE I had borrowed. At first it was like pouring over a volume on nuclear physics, but after another hour or so I started to recognize the main parts from the pictures and was able to vaguely understand what I needed to do to make the camera work.

Fortunately, I'd chosen one that had an automatic setting so I didn't have to worry about fooling around with a lot of dials. Also, it appeared to be already loaded, if I could trust the little window that said 1. That was a real plus, since I couldn't figure out how to open the dumb thing. My only concern now was the size of the snout that stuck out in front. It looked a lot longer than on the cameras I was used to seeing, and it was heavy and kind of awkward. But when I peered through the eye piece everything was greatly magnified and really close, so getting good shots should have been easy.

Finally, I decided I had learned all I could from the manual. Anything else would have to wait until I started using it tomorrow. So I stashed the camera in my school bag, tucked the instruction book in my purse and went downstairs to put the casserole in the oven.

§ § §

Next morning I was up at six-thirty, as usual, and out for my hour of jogging. When I got back, I was surprised to see Judy and the twins already up and eating breakfast. The twins were dressed in identical frothy white blouses, pink gingham pinafores, and pink socks and ribbons. They looked like matching cake decorations.

"What's the occasion?" I asked as I panted into the kitchen and flopped down on a chair across from Judy.

She gave me a long-suffering look and murmured, "Really, Granny, must you come to the table all sweaty? You're making me lose my appetite."

Trixie and Trina looked at each other and started to giggle. Trina made faces at her breakfast and Trixie pinched her nose, but as soon as Judy looked at them they hid their giggles behind their hands.

It was obviously going to be another fun day in the newly-formed Tyler household.

I got up from the table without a word and ran upstairs to shower, my mind full. I was really glad to be in Canada and away from the boring private school I'd been attending nearly as far back as I could remember. But life here was not all *Family Ties*.

Judy was all right, most of the time, but I sometimes felt that I bothered her because I wasn't frilly and feminine. Being feminine is okay, but in my opinion she takes it way too far.

Her main project in life was the twins' career. She was absolutely convinced they were destined to blow their noses on soft tissues and chew sugarless gum on TV before they graduated from kindergarten. I wondered what they thought about it though. Judy had once tried for a career as a model herself and hadn't made it big. I'm sure that was why she was so determined for them. But I felt kind of sorry for them. They didn't seem to have much time for fun, with all their singing and dancing lessons and the way she dragged them from one potential modelling job to another.

By the time I came back downstairs, suitably scented, they were on their way out the door.

"Where are you off to this early in the morning?" I asked as I reached them.

"The girls have a photo date," Judy answered. "There's a new man at Jerome's gallery who is supposed to be fabulous with children. I'm having him do a whole new portfolio."

I stopped and turned to look at her, struck by a sudden thought. "Why don't you just have Father take their pictures? He's the best in the business; I'm sure he could put together a great portfolio of shots just taken here at the house, and you could forget some of these trips to photographic studios."

"Your father is a fine newspaper and magazine photographer," Judy said, "but that kind of work isn't suitable for portraits. I'd never get the girls into the business if I relied on pictures taken around the house. It takes a lot of work to create just the right image." As she spoke she patted Trina's perfectly curled hair and wiped an invisible speck off Trixie's blouse. Then she shooed them both out the door.

"We'll be gone most of the day," she continued as she took a quick look at her own reflection in the hall mirror. "You could put on the roast that's thawing in the sink when you get home." She smiled at me. "And, Granny, why don't you try some of that make-up I gave you last week? A little colour would make so much difference on you."

I didn't say anything, and after a moment's pause she went out. But I looked in the mirror after she had left and wondered if she could be right. I wore no make-up at all. My skin is quite pale except for the freckles, and although my eyes are dark green, I don't have a lot of contrast. Maybe a little make-up would brighten up my face a bit.

But then I pictured the twins' carefully made up faces and shook my head. I'd stay myself for now, thank you very much. Besides, there was too much to worry about that day. Fortunately, it looked like it was going to be a good one for taking photographs.

Chapter 3

The football practice didn't start till one o'clock, so I spent the morning focussing the camera outdoors. By the time I arrived at the field a little after twelve-thirty, I was sure I had it pretty well mastered.

I stationed myself at the fifty yard line to wait for the team to come out. But before the boys showed up, I noticed a gaggle of girls coming onto the field wearing short skirts and twirling batons around. The majorette corps, I cleverly reasoned, and strolled over to where they were getting into formation behind the north goal post.

There were six girls in the corps. As I got close enough, I suddenly realized that Lonnie Kaye and her sidekicks were three of them. I was tempted to turn around and go back to my post at centre field, but I remembered how insistent Steve had been about me getting shots of the majorettes. Now I understood why.

Reluctantly, I continued on until I was within six metres of them. When Lonnie saw me, she pointed and whispered something to the group. Everyone giggled. I mentally willed her baton to bop her on the top of her head, but it didn't work.

The girls started a routine with Lonnie at the head of the group. I raised the camera to focus on her, but all I could see was her stomach. I hadn't had trouble like that when I was focussing on trees and stuff earlier, but I figured things just worked a little differently when you were closer to the subject. The camera would obviously fill in the rest of the picture once I'd focussed on the central part of it. So I took about half a dozen shots, focussing on legs and arms and bottoms and boobs. As I worked I noted on Steve's sheet who was in each shot. I didn't know most of their names, so I just used descriptions.

Finally, the team came on the field and I went down the sideline toward centre field to see what I could catch from there. I was a little farther from the players so the camera showed more of each subject's body, but still I mostly saw either arms or legs as I focussed, not both. As I dutifully recorded the numbers of the players I had shot on my sheet of paper, I wondered how much bigger a field the actual pictures would show.

When the camera didn't wind after I took a picture, I assumed I was out of film. The little window said 36, which seemed to me to be more than enough shots to keep Steve happy. I was beginning to wonder what the big deal was about learning to be a photographer. Things couldn't have been simpler. Now all I had to do was take the film in to be developed on my way home.

Fate, however, decided to get into the act at that point. Just as I started back to the school where I had left my bike, Steve appeared.

"I see you got here bright and early," he remarked, walking toward me with that show-stopping grin. "Get lots of good pictures?"

I paused and waited for him to close in. "I think so," I answered then, trying for a nice balance between confidence and modesty. "I was just about to get them developed."

I turned my head just enough so I could see the majorettes down the field. They had stopped throwing their batons around and were watching us. Good, I thought, and moved a little closer to Steve.

"Fine. I'd like to have them before Monday if possible. I've got a key to the lab, so you can get right at it." He turned and started for the side door of the school.

My God, he expected me to develop the film! And I didn't even know how to take the darn thing out of the camera! In a daze, I followed him into the school and down the hall toward the newspaper office. Maybe if I were lucky the chem lab would blow up, but I didn't hold out much hope.

"Oh, somebody's already here," Steve

remarked as we reached the office. "I guess it must be Gary; he's the only other person with a key. Go right on in, the lab's at the back. Gary can show you where all the materials are." He opened the door and stepped back so I could enter. "I'd stick around, but I've got to pick up Lonnie now. I'll check back in a couple of hours and see what you got." And then he was gone.

I hesitated for a moment to give him time to get out of sight. I could still get out of this mess if I left by the back door and took the film directly to the camera shop. I was just beginning to feel my life wasn't over, when the door to the darkroom opened and Gary came out.

"Hi, Granada," he said easily. "Come to develop the stuff you took at the practice?"

"How did you know I was taking pictures?" I muttered, stalling for time.

"Saw you over at the field when I came down here. I'm finished with my stuff now, and you're welcome to use the chemicals. Come on, I'll show you where everything is."

I had no choice but to follow him. That's when the circus started.

First, I tried to figure out how to get the stupid film out of the camera and, of course, fumbled it.

"Having a little trouble?" Gary asked. "Sometimes the winder on the Nikon can be tricky." He reached out to take the camera. I handed it over without a word.

"Here you are," he said a minute later, and handed me the elusive roll of film. "The pans are over there with the chemicals. The paper is here." He reached up to a shelf and took down a couple of sheets of shiny white stuff. "You'll want to use the contact printing frame, of course. It's over there by the enlarger and the timer."

He might just as well have been speaking Swahili, for all the sense it made to me.

I stood in the middle of the red-lit room, staring around at the tables and praying Gary would suddenly remember a previous engagement for which he was dreadfully late. He didn't. Instead, he parked himself on one of the less cluttered tables and watched me.

I walked slowly over to the pans of liquid on the table and stared down at them. The last time I had felt this ridiculous was when I was eleven and lost the top of my bathing suit at the inter-school mixed diving competition. I didn't have the remotest idea what to do.

Seconds that seemed like hours passed by while I stood motionless. Then the smell of the chemicals and the closeness in the airtight room began to penetrate my brain, and I felt myself begin to sway. I started to fall forward, but before I landed face first in the developing solution, Gary's arms were around me and he was leading me over to the one chair in the room.

"Are you okay?" he asked, an anxious frown on his face.

"I guess so," I murmured, leaning back in the chair and dropping the roll of film on the table beside me. "Boy, it sure is stuffy in here, isn't it?"

"Yeah, sorry about that. The air conditioner isn't working. Look, why don't you go into the office for a breath of air, and I'll develop this for you." He dropped the film in a black bag and took my arm.

I knew I didn't deserve to be let off the hook so easily. Deceiving Steve with Father's pictures was one thing. Girls do that sort of thing all the time in books and always get their man in the end. But thinking I could be a hotshot photographer in one easy lesson was just stupid conceit.

I started to protest, knowing it was time for a little honesty, but Gary wasn't listening. Before I had time to mutter more than a couple of yes but's, he had me bustled right out of the room.

While I sat at one of the desks and waited for Gary to do whatever he was doing, I practised a number of different confessions. Unfortunately, they all made me feel very uncomfortable, like a Class A fool. I shifted around miserably and tried to think of something positive.

Maybe confessing wasn't the best thing to do after all. The film would soon be developed and Gary would never realize I didn't know squat about photography. And telling him the truth now wouldn't really help anything.

I almost had myself convinced until I realized I was getting myself in deeper. I wasn't used to living a lie, and I certainly wasn't enjoying it. I would tell him the truth and throw myself on his mercy. That always works in fiction.

I was feeling almost cheerful when the door shot open and Gary stormed into the room.

"What the hell kind of a joke is this?"

I jumped up and faced him. He was waving a sheet of paper in the air in front of him and practically smoking.

"Is this your idea of high humour, Granada? If so, I don't think Steve will think it's all that funny."

He slapped the sheet down in front of me, and I saw it was covered with a lot of tiny pictures.

"What's that?" I asked in bewilderment. "I thought you were developing my film."

"Of course I was developing your film. That's the contact — " He stopped and stared at me. He didn't say anything for a minute, then his face lost its anger and took on a look of utter contempt.

"You don't know a damn thing about photography, do you?"

"Why on earth would you think that?" I answered, trying to sound a lot more confident than I felt.

"Take a look at those shots," he ordered, handing me a magnifying glass.

Nervously, I took the glass and picked up the paper. I focussed on the first line, scanning it quickly. Then I moved down to the next line, hardly able to believe what I was seeing. There wasn't one complete picture of a player or a majorette in the whole roll. Instead, I had taken thirty-six pictures of appendages and torsos.

I laid the sheet of pictures down on the desk beside me and sort of wilted back into the chair.

"I was going to tell you as soon as you came out of that awful little room," I whispered.

"Yeah, sure you were."

"Honestly." I sat up straight and looked him in the eye.

"Come on, you don't even know the meaning of the word."

Maybe I deserved to get caught out, but I didn't deserve that kind of abuse. I stood up, grabbed the sheet of prints, and ran out of the room.

Gary's voice followed me down the hall. "I should have known you were a phony right away. Those photos you submitted as your own work were just too good for a green kid."

"Green kid, eh," I growled to myself as I peddled home. "We'll see who's a green kid." I promised myself then that I'd become the best darned photographer Fi High had ever seen. Dad would be coming home that evening and I'd get him to start teaching me right away.

Then I remembered that Gary still had my negatives. He'd show them to Steve for sure. And the rest of the student body would probably be let in on the joke before long too. I hadn't been at school for a week yet, and already I'd managed to make myself the resident fool.

That's when I started considering the merits of a long walk on a short pier. After all, four days must rank as a record for the fastest disgraceful end to a promising high school career!

Chapter 4

My thoughts were still black when I reached the house, but as soon as I walked in, they started to brighten. Father was home! I was so glad to see him that for a while I forgot the mess I'd managed to create since he left a week ago. Judy and the children were still at the photographer's, so I had him all to myself until dinner.

At first I managed to get him talking about his latest trip and what he'd seen in South America. But eventually he turned the conversation back to me.

"How was your first week of school, honey?" he asked as I sat on his bed and watched him unpack. "Are you starting to meet lots of kids?"

This, of course, brought back the whole scene in the darkroom and Gary's disgusted face. I could feel my own face begin to crumple as I fought hard not to burst into tears. Father noticed the change immediately.

"What's the matter, Granny? Are you having trouble fitting in?"

"You could say that," I uttered mournfully.

"One week at Fi High and I've managed to totally ruin my life."

Father tried to take my announcement seriously, but his eyes gave him away. "Ah, Granny, it can't be as bad as all that," he managed to say with only a grin. "What horrible crime did you commit anyway?"

He had stopped unpacking and now he sat down on the bed beside me. The sympathetic look I could see behind the laughter was more than I could handle. I broke down and the whole story came pouring out.

When I got to the part about Gary showing me the contact prints of arms and legs, he couldn't control himself any longer. He broke into a roar that could have been heard on the football field.

"You mean you took all your shots with a telephoto lens?" he sputtered between spasms of laughter.

"I don't know what kind of lens it was. I just know it didn't take proper pictures."

He wiped his eyes and shook his head. "Oh, Granny, what a joy you are to have around! To think how much I've missed these last years since your mother died. I wish I could have found a way to keep you with me."

The idea warmed me, but I'm a practical person. "That would have been pretty impossible, Father? Since you were never in one place for more than a few weeks at a time."

"That's true," he sighed. "But still . . ." He broke off and stared into space again. Then, visibly gaining control, he jumped up and rubbed his hands together. "But that's all in the past. We're together now, and the first thing we have to do is see if we can't solve your little problem."

"*Little* problem!" That snapped the warm mood. "Don't you see what will happen when Gary shows Steve those pictures?" I demanded.

"Well, Gran, that's something you're going to have to work out yourself. You'll just have to explain to your editor what you did and try to make him understand why you did it. You never know, he may think it's as funny as I do. As far as I can see, your real problem is persuading him to let you keep your job on the paper. And to do that you're going to have to learn the fundamentals of photography. That's where I can help. Come on, there's no time like the present to start." And without another word, he marched across the room and out the door.

We spent the next two hours in the studio going over the various parts of the camera and what they do. Once I understood the equipment a little better, it wasn't nearly as intimidating as it had been.

We stopped for dinner when Judy and the kids came home a little after five, but we were back again by seven. The rest of the night we worked with various lenses until I couldn't focus my eyes any longer, let alone the camera. Then, in the morning, we started again as soon as Judy had taken the girls to their Sunday dance class. By late afternoon I must have shot ten rolls of film. There were maybe two acceptable pictures in the whole lot, but I was learning fast.

"I'll be home for at least two weeks now, honey," Father said as we finally left the studio, "so we can work together every evening. You'll have to learn your way around the darkroom better, and there's a lot of other technical stuff like the use of filters that we haven't touched yet, but that will all come in good time. For now, what you need is simply a lot of practice."

The marathon lesson had left me exhausted, but I was very happy. And not just because of Father's encouragement either. No, somewhere over the course of the weekend I had discovered something new. I had discovered that photography was really a whole lot of fun!

§   §   §

My life continued to brighten up later that night. Maureen came over after dinner and we went to my room to talk and listen to records. Of course, the first thing she wanted to talk about was my Saturday afternoon shooting session. So I told her what had happened, and she reacted as expected.

"My God, Granny! What have you done? I *told* you you were getting in too deep."

"True, but it's done now. The thing I have to

do is explain the dreadful pictures to Steve and hope he'll give me another chance."

"Why don't you just forget the whole thing and concentrate on an easier mark? There are lots of neat guys in the school. Why zero in on the impossible?"

"Because I think he's the handsomest boy I've ever seen," I replied. "But you're right, I am fighting pretty heavy odds. That's why I need you to help me."

"Me? How? Steve doesn't know I exist."

"No, I mean help me understand how I'm supposed to act and talk and that sort of thing. Father is teaching me to use the camera, so I have that part of the plan taken care of, but I'll need more than that to catch Steve."

Maureen's eyes lit up and she squirmed herself more comfortably into the foam cushions. "Well, great," she approved. "It's about time you started sounding like a fifteen-year-old North American instead of a fifty-year-old European. We'll tackle your vocabulary first. Let's see, I told you about those archaic expressions you're so devoted to, didn't I? Like 'shucks' and 'gee whiz'?" I nodded. "Okay, that's the most important thing. Next, you've got to start calling your father 'Dad'."

I decided it would be a good idea to take notes, so for the next two hours she made suggestions and I wrote them down. When we finally stopped for a junk food break, I had seven pages of instructions. Obviously, this crash course was going to be every bit as difficult as learning photography.

Judy had had a busy weekend with the twins, and the empty cupboards in the kitchen showed it. The only snack food we could find was a box of crackers and some cheese. We reluctantly decided that was better than nothing and sat down at the table to fill in the empty spaces. Neither of us spoke as we tried to imagine we were eating brownies and rocky road ice cream. I guess that's why we were able to hear Dad and Judy so clearly from the living room.

". . . been away and naturally I'm concerned about how she's making out. It can't be easy for her."

"I know, Gordon. I've tried to get closer to her, but it's so difficult. We don't have much in common, and the twins demand so much of my time, we don't get together a lot."

"Judy, I don't mean to interfere — they're your children — but don't you think Trixie and Trina are awfully young to be spending so much time at photo sessions and hairdressers and all the rest of it?"

Judy's voice, which had been barely audible, rose in defense. "There's nothing wrong with the girls getting an early start. With their looks and talent they could have their own TV show in a few years. And while we're thinking about appearances, I want to talk to you about your daughter. She does nothing to make herself attractive."

"There's nothing wrong with Granny's looks, Judy. She's a beautiful girl."

"I know, but she could be so much more, Gordon." Now Judy's voice sounded earnest. "I'm sure I could help her make the most of herself if she'd only let me. After all, I did learn a great deal from that modelling course I took. But she doesn't seem to want to let me help her."

Maureen's face was turning crimson as we listened to this conversation. I suppose mine was even darker.

"Let's take this stuff up to your room," she said abruptly, jumping up from the table and grabbing the box of crackers and the cheese. "We still have a lot to go over."

I mentally thanked her for her diplomatic rescue and followed her out of the room.

It was an hour or so later before Maureen finally ran out of tips. I looked at the sheet of paper in my hand and wondered how I'd ever be able to remember it all. No, tomorrow was the first day of classes — I would need to know it all by then. I didn't want to flub things on my first day. First impressions are so important. Look at the great one I'd made on Gary O'Hare!

"I'll come by and pick you up at eight-thirty," Maureen said as she went out the front door. "We have math together first period, then I'm afraid you're on your own."

"No problem," I answered with more confidence than I really felt. "After the crash course you just gave me, I'm bound to be the most popular kid on the block."

As she walked away, I grinned and gave her a thumbs up sign. But as soon as she was out of sight, I ran back upstairs and spent the next three hours going over my notes. Between this and the camera lessons I might be on my way to sorting my life out, but there was still a lot of work to be done.

Chapter 5

Well, my first day proved conclusively that sorting out your life is not as easy as I had begun to imagine. After Father — Dad — and Maureen spent the weekend with me, I felt a lot less like diving into a bottomless pit. And by the time first period math was over on Monday, I had actually forgotten about Gary and Steve and the photo fiasco and was beginning to feel pretty comfortable.

Then everything started to go downhill.

My next class after math that morning was French. When I went into the room, I saw at once that it was going to be less than chummy. I didn't recognize a soul in there except for Lonnie Kaye Borgnine and her two faithful subjects. That wasn't encouraging, but it wasn't exactly surprising either, since I had been assigned to French III, the grade eleven class, instead of French II with the rest of the sophomores. I must have done well on the test they gave me to determine where I should be placed.

Anyway, I found a seat near the back of the

room and tried not to look uncomfortable. Everyone ignored me entirely, which was just the way I liked it. I determined to remain as invisible as possible and not give Lonnie Kaye any excuse to give me a bad time.

But it was not to be.

We had barely gotten settled after the bell when Madame Rousseau began handing out xeroxed copies of a short story and giving us instructions.

"You will read the story, then answer the questions which follow. Thus, I will determine just how much you comprehend in the French language. It is clear, no?"

A crescendo of groans went up as the class scanned the handouts.

"Silence! You have just one half hour to finish, after which time I will call upon you individually to read your answers. Now begin."

I looked down at the two sheets of paper in front of me and began to grin in relief. It was an excerpt from a De Maupassant story — very easy to translate. I read through it in about five minutes and began to answer the questions. In less than twenty minutes I was done.

I put my pen down and looked around at my classmates. They were all struggling over their papers as though they were trying to break a KGB code. Strange. I glanced up and caught Madame Rousseau glaring unpleasantly at me. I tried smiling at her, but she wasn't about to melt. When the half hour was up, she instructed the class to put down their pens, then turned back to me.

"The oh-so-fast young lady in the green blouse at the back of the second row, you will please read your answer to the first question."

I looked around, saw I was the only one at the back of the class in a green blouse, and stood up. Clearing my throat, I took a deep breath and began to read the paragraph I had written.

I hadn't got more than a sentence or two read when I could feel that something was dreadfully wrong. Kids began to whisper. There was a laugh here, another one over there. I rushed through the remainder of my answer and sat down, bowing my head and pretending to be fascinated with my ballpoint pen while I waited for Madame Rousseau to come down on me. Obviously I hadn't understood the instructions, or maybe it had been the way I read.

The silence from the front of the room was, as they say, deafening. Finally, I couldn't stand the suspense any longer. I looked up, expecting to find Madame Rousseau glaring even more ferociously at me. Instead she was beaming.

"Ah, what a most unexpected pleasure," she laughed. "Your answer, my dear, was quite delightful. And your accent is superb. Yes, quite superb." She laughed again, then turned to a boy in the front row. "Now let us hear how you answered the second question."

The boy stood up and began to stutter his way through a sentence or two, and I finally understood why the class had whispered and laughed when I read my answer. He was replying in English; I had written all my answers in French. My face began to burn. I looked over and saw Lonnie looking back at me. She shook her head disgustedly. Obviously, she thought I'd been showing off, and she was letting everyone know exactly what she thought.

When the bell finally rang to end the class, Madame Rousseau asked me to wait for a moment. After everyone had left, she called me up to her desk and asked me where I had learned to speak such flawless French. I told her about going to school in Europe, where I had been speaking the language since I was seven.

"Ah, I see. Well, there is obviously little I can teach you. I would suggest you transfer to another class. Or, I will give you full credit for French III, and you may use the class time for study period."

I thanked her and said I would see the principal right away. Then, hoping everyone had gone to their next class, I slipped out the door. They hadn't. Lonnie Kaye was standing in the hall with her sidekicks and a bunch of juniors.

". . . such a show-off!" Her voice was loud and angry. "Just because she went to some snooty boarding school in Europe she thinks she can come here and show us up."

She caught sight of me and threw her head back. "Come on, let's get out of here," she motioned to her sidekicks. The rest of the group, carefully avoiding any eye contact with me, quickly moved on to their classes too.

The rest of the morning went without anything else horrible happening. I even began to think that maybe school wouldn't be too bad after all. I wouldn't have to return to French class, and so far my other classes had gone just fine. In one, I'd met a couple of very friendly girls who had invited me to have lunch with them, and we were all heading for the cafeteria when the next bomb exploded.

"Granada." The voice from behind me was one I would have heard in a stadium full of cheering voices.

I turned and saw Steve Williams hurrying toward me.

"Glad I caught you," he panted, while my new friends gazed at me in awe. "Can you come down to the *Speaker* office after school? It's very important that we have a little talk."

My first impulse was to clutch my chest and fake a heart attack, but I don't have Maureen's dramatic talent. Instead, I mumbled something incoherent and backed away from him before he could do any physical violence. He gave me a funny look and repeated the request. "Tonight after school. The *Speaker* office. You *will* come, won't you?"

I nodded mutely. He gave me another strange look, then turned around and walked away.

My two new friends immediately wanted to know how I had managed to capture the interest of the great Steve Williams after one week in school. But I wasn't about to spill the gruesome details, so I shrugged it off and changed the subject. If only they knew how much I wished I *hadn't* captured his interest!

The rest of the day passed uneventfully. I met more kids, found out I was ahead of the class in biology and behind in American lit, and landed a spot as first string forward on the girls' basketball team.

Then it was time to face Steve.

I met Maureen at our lockers after the final bell and gave her a capsule commentary of my day, ending with the royal summons to the *Speaker* office.

"Are you actually going down there?" she exclaimed.

"Of course. I have to explain to him sometime what I did, and today is as good as any other, I guess. I just hope I don't run into Gary O'Hare, that's all. I don't think I could stand to have him see me get reamed out."

She shook her head. "Want me to wait around for you? I could see if the nurse has any spare splints just in case."

"You're very encouraging, Maureen," I

replied, "but you'd better not wait around. I'll probably be quite a while."

As usual, I was wrong.

When I arrived at the *Speaker* office, about ten heads looked up and watched me slip slowly through the door. Fortunately, Gary's wasn't one of them. A low buzz went around the office, and I felt like I was back in French class. Obviously, everybody knew about the disastrous pictures and was waiting to see what Steve was going to do. Well, I'd show them. I'd make him listen to my explanation before he could say anything. I stuck my chin a little higher and marched over to his desk.

"Steve, about those pictures. I'd like to explain what happened."

"Yes, that's what I wanted to talk to you about. I'm giving you a half-page spread. I sure as hell don't know where you came up with that crazy idea, but it works. And as of today you're on the staff of the paper. You'll be Gary's assistant; he'll give you your assignments from now on. Congratulations." He gave me a quick smile, then turned back to the copy he was editing.

I stood perfectly still and stared down at him. Was this some sort of joke that I didn't understand? Maybe this was what hazing was all about. Or was it just Steve's idea of retribution for the mess I'd made of the assignment? I looked around the room expecting to see the rest of the staff convulsed in laughter, but they were all bent over their work and paying no attention to me.

"Was there something else, Granada?" Steve asked when I continued to stand in front of him with my mouth open.

"I don't know why you're doing this," I choked, "but I don't think it's very fair. I'm sorry about the pictures. I came here today to explain, but you didn't even give me a chance." And I whirled and ran out of the room.

I was glad Maureen hadn't waited for me. I hate for anyone to see me cry.

Chapter 6

After I left the *Speaker* office I wept all the way home, then decided I would ask Fa — Dad to send me back to my nunnery in Switzerland. It was perfectly obvious that I couldn't cope in society. The place for me was in the cloistered halls of Mlle. Gagnon's Academy for Young Ladies where there was no Steve Williams, no Gary O'Hare, and, most of all, no drum majorettes. But when I broached the subject, Dad didn't exactly see it with my enthusiasm.

"Honey," he said after he had heard the whole story, "there will always be girls like Lottie Lou or whatever her name is. But running back to your nice safe security blanket in Switzerland won't help you learn how to cope with them. And believe me, most people are pretty nice; you've just had a couple of unlucky starts. Now, let's hear no more about your leaving Canada. I've waited eight years to have you with me, and I'm not about to lose you again." He put his arm around me and kissed the top of my head.

"So, are you ready for your next lesson? I

thought we'd work on people pictures today."

The last thing I wanted to see right at that moment was a camera, but I couldn't hurt his feelings. He was trying so hard to make me feel better. So, reluctantly, I let him steer me to the studio, and for the next couple of hours I got my first lesson in shooting people. And I have to admit that it didn't take more than fifteen minutes before I was hooked again.

But the next day was when things really started to look up for me. Maureen and I were sitting on the front steps of the school eating lunch and trying for an Indian summer tan booster. At least Maureen was; I was eating my sandwich with my head under my sweater and praying no stray sunbeams would find my face. More freckles I didn't need! Anyway, we had stopped talking and were deep in our own thoughts when Toby Tubbs, Maureen's short, bespectacled boyfriend, came out the front door waving a tabloid-sized paper in the air.

"Hey, there you guys are. I've been looking everywhere for you." He peered down at us from the top step. "I brought you a copy of the *Speaker* hot off the press. Thought you might be interested in page two." He grinned knowingly at me and passed down the paper.

I automatically reached to take it, then, realizing what it was, dropped it like it was crawling with maggots. Maureen snatched it up and flipped over the front page. I was furious with Toby for bringing back the memory of that horrible scene with Steve and was about to get up and walk away when Maureen's shriek riveted me to the spot.

"Granny, you got half a page and a big by-line! Wow, I didn't realize you were so good. I guess you were just putting me on about never having used a camera before, eh?"

"You're joking, of course," I muttered, thinking there must be some secret conspiracy to embarrass the new kid. Then I looked down at the page she was holding out to me.

There were six shots laid out in a circular pattern at the top of the page. In the centre was a caption: *Fi High in Motion*. The top picture was a pair of hands catching a football; next came a baton flying in the air with an arm reaching for it; then there was the toe of a boot contacting a football, a pair of arms tackling the lower part of body, another arm firing a pass, and last, but far from least, the upturned back end of a girl reaching for a fallen baton. At the bottom in large letters were the words *Photos by Granada Tyler.*

I couldn't believe what I was seeing. The pictures looked great, nothing like the awful mess that had been on the contact sheet. I remembered I'd shoved the sheet in my bag when I left Gary last Saturday and hadn't looked at it since. I scrambled for it now, and compared it to the pictures in the paper. At first

I couldn't find anything that even remotely resembled the larger pictures. Then, as I started to check each shot carefully, I realized that each of the six pictures in the paper was part of one of my original shots. Someone had apparently cut out the extraneous stuff and left the best part.

Steve. Who else?

He had realized I was a rank amateur and decided to give me a hand instead of reaming me out. Maybe I had made an impression on him after all. I couldn't wait till after school to see him, so I took a chance that he would be in his office during the lunch hour and ran off to check. Maureen's voice followed me up the steps.

"You sure had me fooled, Granny. With that kind of acting talent you should be in the Thespian club instead of wasting your time on the basketball court."

Steve *was* in the office. Unfortunately, so was Gary O'Hare.

"Ah, here's our new star," Steve greeted me as I rushed up to the desk where he was sitting talking to Gary. "How did you like the spread?"

"It was great. That's why I'm down here — I wanted to thank you for fixing it up so well."

"Didn't do a thing. Just put it in the way Gary gave it to me. He even did the circular set-up. Nice, eh?"

"Gary did it?" I stared at him in disbelief.

"Sure, who else? Gary *is* chief photographer.

I turned to Gary and started to smile, but the expression on his face stopped me cold. It was the same disgusted look that I'd seen last Saturday when he realized I was a complete loss with a camera.

Steve seemed oblivious to the uncomfortable exchange. He rattled on about the next edition of the paper which would be coming out in two weeks.

"We're going to do a piece on all the teachers — photo and a bio. Gary will give you your assignment Friday afternoon when we have our bi-weekly planning session." He got up from his chair. "Better get moving, Granada, I think I heard the first bell."

I hung back as Steve grabbed his books and headed for the door. Gary stood up to follow, and I moved into his path so he couldn't pass.

"I don't know what you did to make me look so good, Gary, but I want to thank you. It was really decent of you." I smiled up at him, but I might as well have been trying to charm a bull with a rag. He glared at me and tried to shove past.

"I'm really sorry about the mess I made," I tried again. "I'm taking a crash course in photography and —"

"Look, Granola, or whatever you call yourself, I don't care if you're studying with Ansel Adams. I fixed those pictures up for Steve, not for you. He needed something fast and I couldn't let him down. Unfortunately, we're going to be working on the same paper, but as far as I'm concerned the less we see of each other the better. Now if you'll get out of my way, I'd like to get to class before the next period ends."

I had to either step out of the way or be flattened. I moved, and Gary rushed past me without a second glance.

My mind was definitely not on the life cycle of the salamander as I sat in biology that afternoon. One part of me was ecstatic that I had made a positive impression on Steve Williams. The other part was disgusted that I had done it dishonestly again. But this time it hadn't been my fault; it was Gary who had fixed up my pictures so they looked professional. I had tried to tell the truth, but no one seemed to want to hear it.

That brought me around to Gary and his hostile attitude. Maybe he *did* have a reason to be put off by my initial actions, but he didn't have to treat me like a child molester, for heaven's sake. Working for him would mean that there would be some pretty rough times in my career as girl-photographer. Still, I would be seeing Steve nearly every day, and I would make him learn to appreciate me for what I really can do, not for something Gary did to make me look good.

That meant a real commitment to my work with Dad. I'd study hard, read everything I could find in his library, and work like crazy to be the best photographer Fi High ever saw. Maybe I'd have to take orders from the great Gary O'Hare for a while, but give me a few months and I'd make him look like a six-year-old with a Baby Brownie.

I couldn't wait until school was out so I could get home to the camera Dad had loaned me and my next lesson on the road to the cover of *Time*!

Chapter 7

"There are many factors to be considered when you're taking pictures of people, Granny," Dad said later that afternoon as he checked my camera to make sure I'd loaded it properly. "But by far the most important is action. You'll have to learn about lighting, indoor and outdoor, and perspective and so forth, but no one can teach you to see a great action shot. It's something you have to develop for yourself."

"Do you mean I have to take pictures of people running or jumping all the time?"

"No, of course not. By action shot I mean your subject should be doing something that speaks to the viewer. A little child standing perfectly still watching a spider spinning a web is an action shot. There are great pictures just waiting to be taken everywhere you look, honey. But you've got to keep your camera eyes open.

"Okay," he handed me the camera, "now let's go over to the park and see what we can get. We still have an hour or so of good light."

I shot two rolls of film that afternoon, black and white of course. At first I thought Dad made me shoot black and white because it was cheaper, but he soon straightened me out on that score.

"Colour is great, Granny, but anybody can make a pretty picture with colour. It takes a true artist to make a great black-and-white photo. Besides, colour is more difficult to process, and you're going to be doing all your own developing. That's half the art."

When we got to the park, the first thing that caught my eye was a group of kids playing on the swings and teeter-totters. I shot a whole roll of them, then we went down to the lagoon where I tried a few shots of a little girl wading in water up to her skirt and looking for shells. There were some people windsurfing farther out, but I didn't have a telephoto lens so I couldn't even try for them. Dad insisted I use only a regular 55 mm lens until I had it mastered. Wide angle and telephoto lenses would come later.

I finished off my second roll with some pictures of a baby playing with a stuffed animal, then we drove home. I wanted to start developing them right away, but when we got into the house Judy was in quite a state.

"Oh, good, you're back. Granny, could you give me a hand? I'm running late."

"Sure, Judy. What do you want me to do?"

"You could make a salad for starters, then set the table. I've been going like crazy all day, and I just got home. I had to pick up the proofs of the girls' photos, which, incidentally, were terrible. I'm going to have him do them all over again. Then there was the girls' dancing lesson, and Trina had an appointment for . . ."

I turned her off as she continued to review her day, and went to the kitchen to start on the salad. Dad, I noticed, headed for his den as soon as we got in the door. Both of us knew what Judy was like when a setback disturbed the twins' career. She wouldn't stop talking about them now until the full load of her disappointment had been worked out — and with terrible proofs that could take a while.

We listened to her rattling on about the faults of the new photographer all through dinner. Fortunately, most of it was drowned out by the chattering and bickering of the girls who, when their mother wasn't busy turning them into models, were just as boisterous as any other five-year-olds. I wondered again why Judy couldn't see that that was really when they were at their best.

As soon as dinner was over and the dishes done, Dad and I slipped out to the studio to develop the shots I had taken. A few of them weren't bad, but most really showed what an amateur I was. One shot of a kid on a teeter-totter broke me up. It looked like he had a lamppost growing out of his left shoulder.

"Every budding photographer comes up with a version of that," Dad informed me when

I had finished chuckling. "It happens when you're not looking at the whole picture. After all, the lens is just a piece of equipment; it can't decide what should or shouldn't be in the shot."

A lot of the shots were blurred or out of focus or else badly centred, but a couple were pretty good. I had caught the little wader just as she spotted a prize shell, and the expression on her face was great. And one of a kid on a swing was also quite passable.

"Not bad for a beginner," Dad announced when we had checked the contact sheet with a magnifying glass. "We'll crop these two a little, then blow them up."

That's when I had my first lesson in what the darkroom can do to fix up your mistakes. By the time it was through I was even able to understand what Gary had done to make those six pictures of arms and legs come out looking downright professional.

We finished up about eight-thirty and went back into the house. Trixie and Trina had gone to bed, and Judy was sitting across the room with a froth of pink lace on her lap. When she saw us, she jumped up and ran into the dining room. She was back almost instantly with a handful of pictures.

"Gordon, I want you to look at what that man did to the girls." She handed him the proofs with an angry flourish and threw herself back into her chair.

Dad studied the pictures for a couple of minutes, then handed them back to her.

"It's not the photographer's fault entirely, Judy," he began. "The girls look so unnatural with that make-up, and their smiles are posed. If he had given them something to play with it might have relaxed them."

"Oh, he suggested that, but I wanted them to look professional, not like a couple of ordinary little children playing with dolls. After all, Gordon, these photos are supposed to be for the modelling agency."

"Suit yourself, Judy, but remember, they *are* children. And that's what the modelling agency will be looking for. I still think you should go easy on the make-up."

Judy didn't answer, but it was pretty obvious she wasn't buying it. She picked up the material she had been working on and started to sew again.

"What are you making?" I asked, more to change the subject than out of any real interest.

"It's a dress for Trixie. I want to have it done before the girls go back to have their pictures redone. Trina's is already finished. Would you like to see it?"

"Sure," I agreed.

"Great!" She jumped up and left the room. A minute or two later she was back with a frothy blue article over her arm. She held it up for me to see and I kind of gasped.

"Judy, that's a formal gown. Don't you think maybe it's a little old for Trixie?"

"No, of course not." She looked from me to Dad, then continued. "You just don't understand the modelling business, either of you. If the girls are going to get to the top, they have to make the most of their potential."

"I see," I muttered, not seeing at all. In my opinion it was time she opened her eyes and started to see a few things herself. But I bit my tongue and said nothing.

"Well, good luck with other dress," I finally managed to say carefully. "I'm going upstairs to call Maureen now."

I had to bring Maureen up to date on the latest in the ongoing Steve-Granny drama. I hadn't had a chance earlier to tell her the truth about the photos, or what Steve had said about putting me on staff permanently.

"You rushed off so fast after you saw the paper, Granny. What was it all about anyway?" Maureen's voice was full of concern.

"It's a long story, Morrie, both good and bad, but the gist of it is that I'm on the paper permanently. That's the good part. The bad part is that I have to take orders from that arrogant little pipsqueak, Gary O'Hare."

"Pipsqueak? Oh, Granny, where did you get that one from? She started to laugh.

"Not cool?" I enquired.

"Definitely not cool. Anyway, what hap-

pened to make you think Gary's a pipsqueak?"
She snorted again.

So I told her the whole gruesome story of what had happened with my first assignment, and how Gary had been so disgusted with me. And how he had then turned around and made me look so good.

"I tried to apologize and explain it all to him, but he wouldn't even give me the time of day. He just walked out on me. Anyway, it doesn't matter; I'm going to beat him at his own game. Dad's teaching me how to use the camera properly now. Give me a few weeks and we'll see who sneers at whom."

"I can't understand Gary acting like that. Toby thinks he's a great guy. They've done a few assignments together, and Toby says he's the easiest person in the school to work with."

I'd forgotten that Maureen's boyfriend was also on the staff of the *Speaker*. That made two people there who were on my side. Maybe my career as a girl photographer wouldn't be as rough as I'd thought.

"Look, Maureen, I'm going to need a lot of practice taking photos of people. How would you like to be my model? When I get really good you can use the stuff I shoot for publicity pictures to get your career rolling."

"Get serious!" she shouted into the phone. "I'll have a whole portfolio by the time I'm ready to go professional."

The word portfolio brought the whole business of Judy and the twins back to me, and I shuddered. No way would my pictures of Maureen look like the ones that photographer had taken of Trixie and Trina. I remembered what Dad had said about letting them play with something to relax them, and wondered if Maureen would agree to have her picture taken in the tub with a rubber duckie.

"What's so funny?" she demanded when that arresting vision had taken over my brain. "I *am* going to go professional, you know. In fact, I've already decided what my stage name will be." She paused for dramatic effect. "Moonlit Forest," she breathed. "How do you like it?"

I pretended to consider the suggestion while I got myself under control. "Hmm, Maureen Chase — Moonlit Forest; yes, I see. It's quite unusual, Morrie. A name no one will forget."

"And they won't forget me either," she announced. "Just wait till I get these braces off my teeth and have my hair lightened. I'm going to try out for the lead in the Christmas play and I'm going to get it. You'll see."

I smiled to myself. If anyone could make it, Maureen could. I only hoped I would be as successful in my effort to beat Gary out as chief photographer for the paper.

"I know you will," I answered her. "See you tomorrow." Then I hung up and lay back on my bed to think.

The first planning session of the *Speaker* staff was on Friday. I'd be pleasant and agreeable and do everything Gary asked me to do. He'd have no reason to complain to Steve about me, and I'd do such a great job he'd have to recognize my talent. Then it would be just a matter of time before Steve began to appreciate me too. Things were definitely starting to look up for Granny Tyler.

Chapter 8

The next five days were right out of SweetValley High. Didn't someone once say that life reflects art? Well, I'm here to tell you it's absolutely true.

I really began to study photography in earnest, reading everything I could get my hands on and shooting every afternoon, either alone or with Dad. I won't go into the curriculum, but I honestly believe that I could have written my own book on photography. Of course, I wasn't a great photographer yet, but I sure did know the technical side of taking and developing pictures.

On Friday, I met with the staff of the Speaker and received my next assignment from Wary Gary. Honestly, you'd think I was completely incapable of focussing a camera and pushing the button, the way he treated me. We were going to run a spread on the staff, and Gary had to provide shots of each of the teachers, preferably in action. I naturally supposed we would divide the staff in two; it seemed the sensible thing to do. But no, Gary gave me three teachers to photograph and assigned himself the other twenty-two.

"And I want to see what you've got by Wednesday, Granada," he warned me as we were getting up from the meeting, "in case I have to re-shoot your stuff."

I was so angry I wanted to punch him right in his F-stop, but I restrained myself and moved away before I did anything I might regret later. Besides, Steve was getting ready to leave, and I wanted to arrange it so we went out of the room together.

It worked out beautifully too. We just naturally fell into step as we headed for our lockers, and after congratulating me again on the unique job I'd done on the Fi High in Motion layout, he asked me if I had a ride home.

"No, I don't," I answered from somewhere in outer space. Actually, I had my bike, but he didn't need to know that. I'd have to walk to school the next day, but that was a small sacrifice to make for ten minutes alone with Steve Williams.

"Come on then, my car's parked at the back. We can stop on the way for a Coke, if you'd like, and you can tell me where you learned your way around a camera."

He walked and I floated out the door and across the parking lot.

We drove to a pizza place which I didn't know existed, a good kilometre from the school.

I wondered if maybe he was going out of his way not to be seen with me in case it got back to Lonnie Kaye, and for a moment the excitement I'd been feeling turned to gloom. But as soon as we went in the door I realized how mistaken I had been. The place was crowded with students, mostly seniors as far as I could judge. Steve led me to an empty booth at the far end of the room and asked me what I wanted.

"Whatever you're having will be fine," I answered, wishing there were some way I could take a picture of the two of us sitting together, for posterity and the front page of the Speaker.

The waitress came over and he ordered two Cokes and two slices of pizza — double cheese and lots of pepperoni, just the way I like it. Then he settled back against the partition between booths and smiled.

"Okay, so how did you get so good with a camera? Did you take photography at that girls' school?"

"Not exactly," I hedged, wondering if this was the time and place to make my confession. But before I had a chance to decide, a familiar voice came floating toward us from the front of the room. Lonnie Kaye's pink sweater followed it.

"Steve, what on earth are you doing here? I thought you had a *Speaker* meeting." She was standing over us, staring at Steve and completely ignoring me.

Steve looked up with a sheepish grin and said, "We finished a little earlier than I expected and since Granny didn't have any way to get home I offered her a lift. She was hungry, so we stopped here to grab a quick pizza."

I was hungry? That was news to me. But I could see why Steve had made up the story. Lonnie's eyes were shooting flames that threatened to send the whole place up in smoke.

"Well, if you think you can tear yourself away, you did promise to come over to the house and help me set up my new stereo."

At that moment the waitress came with our order. Steve looked from Lonnie to the hot pizza, then back at Lonnie again. The pizza won.

"Just let me finish this, then I'll be right with you," he told her. He took a big bite and washed it down with a swig of Coke. "I'll have to take Granny home first though, but it won't be out of the way. Will it?" he turned hopefully to me.

"I live on Brandfort Crescent," I supplied.

"Oh, great!" Lonnie sighed. "Just the opposite direction."

Steve looked so upset as he shifted his gaze from her to me that I felt I had to take him off the hook.

"It's okay," I assured him, "I can walk it. In fact, I'll enjoy the exercise; I didn't get my jogging in this morning."

"Oh, God, wouldn't you know. She jogs too!"

Steve didn't say anything. His mouth was full and his eyes were on his glass.

I took a last bite from my pizza and finished my Coke. "Thanks for the snack, Steve. I'll be on my way." I stood up and waited for a moment to see if Steve would insist on driving me home. But he didn't, so I walked quickly to the front of the cafe and out the door.

The last thing I heard as the door swung shut behind me was Lonnie's voice complaining, "Honestly, Steve, I don't know why you insist on collecting all these stray losers. Couldn't you maybe settle for an abandoned kitten?"

It took me half an hour to walk home, and by the time I arrived I had worked my way into a seething rage at Lonnie Kaye Borgnine. Not only had she ruined my semi-date with Steve, but she had insulted and embarrassed me in front of thirty people. Just because I was having an innocent pizza with her boyfriend.

Okay, maybe it wasn't so innocent. But after all, all's fair in love and war, and she certainly didn't own him. Besides, she was cruel and mean-minded; she deserved to lose him. At least, that's what I tried to convince my annoying conscience, which persistently imagined a look of hurt on her face when she'd first seen me with Steve.

By the time dinner was over and Dad and I were back in his studio, I had decided to forget about Lonnie Kaye and worked up a good head of steam about Gary O'Hare and his condescending attitude that afternoon.

"I know I made a mistake, Dad, and I'm sorry for it, I really am. But he just won't accept it. He gave me an assignment today that was almost an insult."

Dad was fitting a large lens on my camera and peering through the eye piece.

"It doesn't matter what the assignment is, honey," he assured me. "The important thing is to do a good job. Now I want you to try this out. It's called a zoom lens. It lets you shoot from various distances without having to change lenses." He handed the camera to me and continued.

"It's not that different from a regular 55 millimetre lens — you focus and push the button. But the point you have to remember with this lens is that you adjust it to bring your subject as close as you want in order to fill the frame, then focus. Not the other way around."

I took the camera, which now seemed about ten times heavier, and peered through the viewfinder. All I could see was a dark blur. But when I rotated the lens, the door handle across the room jumped up at me. Then I extended the lens and it receded back.

"Hey, this is great!" I exclaimed. "I can shoot from anywhere and not have to worry about subject to camera distance."

"It should be very helpful when you're

taking candid shots for the paper, Granny. Now, let's go back to the park and see what you can do with it."

We stayed until the light was too faint to shoot, then came home and developed the roll I'd taken.

"Some of these are very good, honey," Dad exclaimed as he scanned the contact sheet. "You're getting a real feel for composition, and you seem to have got the hang of proper focussing. I see no reason why you can't take candid shots of your teachers that will please even your arch enemy." He grinned at me as he passed the sheet over.

They were good, too. I guess all that practice and studying had paid off. Or maybe I just inherited Dad's photography gene. Anyway, I decided I would spend the weekend shooting with the zoom lens so that by Monday I'd be ready to get some super shots of the three teachers I'd been assigned. I'd taken so many pictures of Maureen in the last three days that I didn't think I could bear to see her face through the lens again for a while. So who would I shoot over the weekend?

I was still pondering the various possibilities when the answer barrelled into me. Literally. Dad and I had just gone back into the house when Trixie and Trina came roaring out of the kitchen right into us. They were in their sleepers and had their faces freshly washed, and they looked so cute and natural that my mind was made up. I'd spend the weekend getting candid shots of the twins.

And I did. It worked out perfectly. Judy and Dad went off together to Washington to do some shopping and see a show. They left me to babysit until Sunday evening, which made everything easier. I wasn't sure how Judy would react to me photographing the girls in their normal state, but what she didn't know wouldn't hurt her. And I needed the practice with the zoom lens.

As soon as we had the house to ourselves, I got Trixie and Trina into their bathing suits and took them out to the back yard. I turned the sprinkler on, settled myself behind the rail on the back porch, and got my camera ready. I shot two full rolls before they got tired and wanted to come in for a snack. I got another roll of them in the tub together that night, and in the morning I caught them coming downstairs still half asleep, wearing their nighties and clutching their identical stuffed elephants. We went over to the park in the afternoon, and I finished another two rolls of them playing in the sandbox.

When Dad and Judy came home at six, I'd managed to get over two hundred pictures of the girls at their best. I couldn't wait to develop them.

Chapter 9

But Monday morning I had to forget about the girls' photos; I had bigger things to deal with first. I took the camera and zoom lens to school and started taking my candid shots of the teachers.

I was assigned Mr. Froes, the biology teacher, Ms. Hackett, girls phys ed, and Mrs. Scotia, the queen of family studies in the home ec kitchen. It was no picnic trying to catch them in action, since I had to be in class most of the day and could only work during study period, but I managed to finish a roll of film by Tuesday afternoon.

When I started to develop the pictures that evening, I was pretty shaky. What if I didn't get one decent shot out of the whole thirty-six? How could I ever face Gary O'Hare and admit he was right about me? But I didn't need to worry. When I had printed the contact sheet, I gave it a quick look with the magnifying glass and saw that at least half a dozen shots were okay. Dad came in while I was scanning the sheet more closely and asked how they were.

"Here, take a look for yourself. I think I'll be able to salvage at least one good shot of each of the teachers."

He took the magnifying glass from me and studied the sheet carefully. I held my breath until he finally looked up with a grin.

"Other than the fact that you didn't get some of them focussed sharply enough and the composition of a few of the others leaves a bit to be desired, I'd say you did just fine." He handed the sheet back to me and smiled. "Which ones are you going to print?"

I looked at the tiny pictures again and answered hesitantly. "I think the one of Mr. Froes holding up the frog by one leg is pretty good. And I like this one of Ms. Hackett tying her running shoes, but it's kind of off-centre."

"No problem, you can crop it. What about this other woman?"

"Mrs. Scotia. She's the home ec teacher, in case you didn't guess," I giggled. "What do you think of the one where she's glaring down at the burnt muffins?"

"I think it's excellent. You've really caught the spirit of the candid shot. I hope your teachers have a good sense of humour though," he laughed as he got up to leave.

"You're going to stick around and help me, aren't you?" I cried.

"Nope, you're on your own now. You know what to do; just go ahead and do it. Bring the prints in when you've finished." And giving me a pat on the shoulder, he left the studio.

It took me about twice as long as it should have to set up the enlarger and crop the shot of Ms. Hackett. I was so anxious to do a perfect job that I kept messing up. Finally I managed to get three decent prints just as Dad came back.

"I thought you might have fallen into the developing solution and drowned," he chuckled as he came over to where I was hanging the wet prints up to dry. "Hey, those look all right," he nodded encouragingly, then started to sort through a stack of contact sheets that were sitting on the table beside the enlarger.

I didn't pay too much attention to what he was doing. I was far too concerned about the shots I had just blown up. Could they be too informal? Is that what Dad meant when he said he hoped the teachers had a sense of humour? But Gary had told me to get candid shots, and that's what I'd done. If he didn't like them, he could darn well shoot them himself.

Unfortunately, that was exactly what I didn't want to happen.

I was wondering if I should try to take another roll the next morning, skip afternoon classes to develop them, and get them back in time for the after school deadline, when Dad's voice started to penetrate.

"Granny, when did you take these pictures of the twins?"

"Saturday and Sunday while you and Judy were out of town. I was practising with the zoom lens. I made the contact prints right away, but I haven't had time yet to even take a good look at them. I bet they're pretty awful."

"On the contrary, you've got some exceptional shots here. Would you mind if I blew a few of them up?"

"No, of course not. But they're probably not very good. I was just enjoying myself and trying to get the feel of the camera, so I was pretty casual about what I took."

He didn't bother to comment. "Where are the negs?" he asked, looking around.

"In that cupboard over there, I think," I answered absently, once again studying my prints. They were dry now, so I took them down from the line and put them carefully into a brown envelope.

"Do you really think these are okay, Dad?" I pleaded for reassurance.

"What?" He looked vaguely at me from over by the cupboard. "Oh, yes, your school assignment. They're just fine, Granny, and don't you let anyone tell you they're not."

But it didn't take long for someone to do exactly that.

I took the prints down to the *Speaker* office right after school the next day and handed them over to Gary. He barely glanced at me, then turned back to his own work and muttered,

"Just put them down. I'll check them later."

I held onto my temper with difficulty, but I wasn't about to leave until he'd seen them and made a decision. So I wandered over to where Toby was banging away on an old manual that was probably conceived before he was.

When I stopped at his desk, he raised his head and beamed metallically up at me. He wears braces identical to Maureen's, which apparently has led to some interesting consequences.

"Honestly, Granny," Maureen had confessed one day the week before, "it's so embarrassing. Every time we kiss we pick up the all-news radio station."

Her words came back to me as his braces glinted in the light, and I started to laugh.

"You're in a happy mood, Granny," he commented. "Got your assignment in okay?"

That effectively killed the laughter. I nodded dejectedly.

"Gary has it on his desk, but he hasn't deigned to look at it yet."

"He's pretty busy. We have to have all the copy in by Friday now, you know. The printer who does our work has moved the deadline up, and it means everyone has to work like crazy."

Before I could make the appropriate sympathetic noises, Steve came into the room and my mind went into overdrive.

"Granny, just the girl I want to see," he

called from the door. "Come over here for a sec, will you?"

He walked to his desk, and I dutifully followed.

"Look, I'm really sorry about last Friday," he began as he seated himself across from me. "I hope you didn't mind walking home. You see, I'd sort of promised Lonnie and —"

"That's okay," I assured him, delighted that he had been concerned. "Maybe we can do it again sometime." Nothing like taking the bull by the horns.

He looked startled for a moment, then nodded. "Sure, why not?" As I struggled to control the flush I was sure was starting to cover my face, he continued. "Did you get your assignment done, Granny? You've heard about our new deadline, haven't you?"

"Yes, Toby just told me about it. Gary has my work on his desk. He hasn't opened it yet."

"Well, let's take a look at it." He got up, and again I followed behind him as he strolled over to Gary's desk.

He opened the brown envelope, took out the three prints, and started to roar with laughter.

"Hey, these are terrific, Granny! How did you ever catch such great poses?"

"Well, I just went into their classes whenever I had a free period and waited till I thought I had a good shot. Do you like them?" I asked timidly.

"Like them? I love them. Here, Gary, take a look at these."

Gary, who had been studiously ignoring this whole exchange, raised his head with a sigh and reached for the pictures.

He stared at them for a minute, then looked up at Steve.

"You're not seriously thinking of printing these, are you?"

"Of course. Why not?"

Gary threw them down on the desk and snorted. "Well, it's up to you; you're the editor. But I want it understood here and now that I'm having nothing to do with them." Without another word, he picked up his marking pencil and turned back to his work.

I could feel the anger that he always seemed to be able to create well up in my stomach. "Are they really as bad as all that, Mr. Yousuf Karsh, or is it that they're too good?"

"What the hell are you talking about?" He glared up at me.

"Just that you're very quick to put down my work, even though Steve thinks it's fine. Or do you think you know more than he does?"

He gave me a disgusted look, then turned to Steve. "Take her away, will you? I'm too busy to trade insults with a conceited beginner."

Steve took my arm and led me back to his desk. Everyone in the room was looking at me, and I could feel the old flush starting again.

"It's okay, Granny," Steve soothed when we were out of earshot. "Gary sometimes get like that under pressure. Now, about that raincheck. How about meeting me tomorrow after school?"

"Great!" I answered, my anger with Gary completely forgotten. "But won't you be pretty busy putting the paper together?"

"Not too busy to break for an hour." He smiled and waved me out. "Now disappear. I've got a lot of work to do."

As I turned to leave, I saw Gary watching me. He didn't look angry or even disgusted. The word that came to mind to describe him was disappointed.

I couldn't have been happier.

Chapter 10

Thursday morning Maureen was waiting for me at the corner as usual. She'd been out with Toby the night before, so I hadn't had a chance to tell her about my forthcoming date with Steve. But before I could get launched on my story, she started right in.

"Toby told me about what happened yesterday afternoon, Granny," she announced as she jumped on her bike. "Boy, you really know how to live dangerously, don't you?"

"What do you mean?" I hedged, wondering how she could have found out so soon. Maybe Toby had overheard Steve ask me out. "She doesn't own him, you know."

"Who doesn't own who? What are you talking about?"

"Whom," I corrected automatically. "Lonnie doesn't own Steve. Isn't that what you meant by living dangerously?"

"No, of course not. I meant taking on Gary O'Hare. He's a great guy, but he's got a temper like a lit firecracker. It's his red hair, I guess," she added, then looked stricken. "Oh, I'm sorry!

I don't mean all redheads have violent tempers, Granny. I —"

"It's okay, I have been known to get a little huffy at times."

She grinned. "I just can't understand why Gary didn't cream you on the spot for accusing him of being jealous of your work. He's verbally massacred people for much less."

"He's an egotistical old poop, Maureen, and he deserved whatever I gave him."

"An old poop," she hooted, loosing her balance and nearly wiping out a lamppost. "I haven't heard that since I was in kindergarten."

"Well, he is," I countered. We had arrived at the school and were locking our bikes in the rack. "Let's forget about Gary O'Hare, Maureen. I've got more important things to tell you. Steve asked me out for a Coke after school today. Isn't that smashing?"

Maureen snapped her padlock shut and shook her head.

"You really do like to live dangerously, don't you? Just wait till Lonnie Kaye hears about that."

But there was no way Lonnie Kaye would ever hear about that date unless either Steve or I told her.

As soon as the final bell went, I rushed to my locker and down to the *Speaker* office. Steve was already out in the hall waiting. As soon as he saw me he ran up, grabbed my arm and rushed me out the back door to his car. Then we drove all the way downtown to a little hamburger joint on Main Street. Needless to say, there wasn't anyone from Fineacres High anywhere nearby.

We sat down, ordered burgers and milkshakes, and looked at each other. For the first time in my life I wished I had more than a passing acquaintance with eye shadow and lip gloss. However, Steve didn't seem to mind the naked face across from him. He started to quiz me about my photographic skills again, but I managed to detour him onto the paper and school, and then he spent the rest of the time telling me what he was going to do when he graduated in June. I sat in total dumb silence and palpitated.

After half an hour that seemed to go by in fifteen seconds, he picked up the bill and said he would have to get back to the office. He'd be working till midnight at least.

I waited till we were back in his car, then asked if there was anything I could do to help.

"Nope, unless you know anything about layout. And if I remember correctly from our first meeting, you don't."

For a split second I considered telling him I had practically been weaned doing layouts, but then I remembered what the last little deception had gotten me.

"No, I'm afraid not. But I could learn."

"Maybe another time, when we're not so busy," he answered, his mind obviously on other things.

We drove back to the school without exchanging another word, but that was just fine with me. It gave me a chance to watch his Tom Cruise profile as he steered the car through the rush hour traffic.

§   §   §

Nothing of any great importance happened for the next few days. The paper got put to bed on Friday without my help, Dad went on another assignment on Saturday, and I spent the entire weekend down at Stanley Park taking pictures of strangers. There was no school on Monday, so I was free to develop my stuff and blow up the best shots for Dad to see when he came home.

Then came Tuesday. That was the day I decided that maybe it would be best if I just gave up trying to be a photographer and went into something less traumatic, like sky-diving.

Maureen and I were getting into the cafeteria line-up when one of the freshmen who hangs around the *Speaker* office came in with a stack of papers hot off the press. I rushed over, grabbed a copy, and started to flip through the pages. True to his plan, Steve had devoted the whole middle section to pictures of the faculty. Most of the shots showed teachers at their desks or writing on the blackboard or lecturing. Good candid shots, all of them. Then there were the three I had contributed. It wasn't until I saw them in conjunction with Gary's pictures that I realized why he had been so hostile. They were completely different, and a lot more interesting.

It wasn't so much that the pictures were taken under unusual circumstances; it was the expressions on the faces. Mr. Froes appeared to be ready to throw up as he held the wiggling frog by its leg, and Mrs. Scotia was viewing the burnt muffins with a look that clearly said, "How could this disgusting mess ever have happened to me?" As for Ms. Hackett, what you could see of her face showed strained determination. You see, I had shot her from behind, and her head appeared between her rather hefty thighs as she bent over to tie her shoes.

The paper hit the halls at noon, and by twelve-thirty everyone in the school was talking about my photos. No one knew who had taken them, but they all assumed it was Gary. Maureen was quick to straighten out that little piece of misinformation though. By the first bell people were coming up to me and congratulating me on giving the paper a little pizzazz.

I enjoyed the attention, of course, but I began to be a little concerned about how the three teachers would take the whole thing. Come to think of it, fun-loving was not a term that sprang immediately to mind when I thought of them. And fun was definitely what the students were having with those photos. On the other hand, Steve would never have printed them if he had thought they would really upset anyone.

I had just about convinced myself that I'd done a good job and that the kids were right. The shots did give the paper some pizzazz, a lot more than Gary's ordinary pictures did. Then, in the middle of math class, everything hit the fan.

"Mr. Goth, please send Granada Tyler to the office immediately." Mr. Lambert's voice left no room for doubt that immediately meant right now.

Mr. Goth nodded to me, and I hurried out of the room.

When I got to Mr. Lambert's office, the secretary motioned for me to go right in. She was trying to look stern, but her lips kept twitching and she suddenly needed to cough into her hanky. It was all very unnerving.

Mr. Lambert was sitting behind his desk doing a much better job of looking stern. Seated in a semi-circle in front of him, their backs to me, were my three subjects. Steve was slumped in a chair by the wall, looking uncomfortable.

"Come in, Miss Tyler," Mr. Lambert ordered.

As I stood in front of his desk waiting for him to speak, he reached into his desk drawer, removed a copy of the *Speaker* opened at the centre, and placed it in front of me.

"Are you responsible for these pictures?" he demanded.

"Just three of them," I answered. I didn't think it was necessary to point out which three — Froes, Hackett and Scotia were snarling in unison behind me.

"Just what did you think you were doing?"

"I was told to take candid shots and that's what I did."

"Candid? Insulting would be a better word, don't you think?"

"I — I didn't mean to —"

"I don't know what you did or didn't mean. The point is that you have embarrassed three of our most respected teachers. What do you propose to do about it?"

I looked at the trio. They glared back. I shifted my gaze to Steve, and he started to stand up.

"Look, Mr. Lambert, don't blame Granada. I'm the editor; the responsibility is mine."

"True enough, Mr. Williams, and I'll deal with you later. In the meantime, please sit down and be quiet."

Steve gave me a sympathetic look, shook his head, and slumped back into his chair.

"Now, Miss Tyler, you haven't answered my question. What are you going to do about this most unfortunate situation?"

"I don't know. What do you want me to do?" My voice was sounding pretty shaky. I felt like a double agent who had just got caught with a shoe full of microfilm.

"First, I would suggest that you apologize to the teachers you have so thoroughly insulted."

He sat back and waited while I faced the hostile trio and stumbled my way through three "I'm awfully sorry's." When each of my victims had grudgingly acknowledged my apology, he continued.

"Second, you will stay after school and write a five-hundred word essay on consideration. You will continue to remain after school until the essay is done to my satisfaction.

"Third, you may consider yourself banned from all extra-curricular activities for the next two weeks."

"Does that include working on the Speaker?" I asked innocently.

He nearly put his fist through the desk.

"It most certainly does. In fact, you may consider yourself off the paper for good."

I looked over at Steve again. He was sitting bolt upright and looked like he'd been zapped by an alien life form.

"But, sir, Granada is the best photographer we've ever had on the paper. She —"

"We will not discuss this any further. You may return to your classes, and I will see you here in my office at four o'clock, Mr. Williams."

I almost expected him to say "Case dismissed," but he merely wobbled his chins at us and turned back to the trio in front of him.

I got out of there in about five seconds flat,

and Steve was only a few seconds behind.

"Gee, Granny, I'm really sorry about that. I guess I never should have printed those pictures you submitted, but they were so darned good I couldn't resist." He looked down at me with concern.

"It's okay, Steve, it wasn't your fault. I guess I should have known better. But thanks for trying to help. Are you going to get in a lot of trouble over this?" I asked, raising my eyes to look at him.

"Naw. He'll give me a lecture, threaten to take away my job, then forget about it." He smiled and took my arm. "There's only ten minutes left in the period, no point going back to class. Let's go down to the office; it should be empty this time of day."

"I suppose you know how much I'll miss the paper," I said as we approached the office door. I bent my head so he wouldn't see the tears I could feel welling up in my eyes.

"And I hate losing you. You're the best photographer we've ever had."

"Better than Gary?"

"Well, more original, that's for sure."

Suddenly the whole fiasco faded from my mind. Steve thought I was a great photographer. More original than his precious Gary O'Hare.

Then it hit me. How did Lambert know that I had taken the shots that had offended him so? Both my name and Gary's were under the layout, but we weren't identified with any particular photo. It must have been Gary. He had figured there would be trouble and had made darn sure that Lambert and the three teachers knew exactly who was responsible. Suddenly I was so mad I could have cheerfully stuffed the enlarger down his throat.

At that moment Gary himself stepped out of the darkroom carrying a bunch of negatives.

"Well, I hope you're satisfied," I exploded as he came toward us.

"What are you talking about?"

"You couldn't wait to get to Lambert, could you?"

He turned to Steve. "Do you know what she's babbling about?"

Steve nodded. "Yeah, Lambert kicked her off the paper."

"Off the paper? Why?"

"Oh, c'mon now, don't pretend you don't know. It was those pictures of the teachers." I could feel the tears collecting again. I had to get out of there before they overflowed.

As I walked out of the room, I could hear Gary still asking Steve, "But why the hell is she so mad at me?"

What a creep!

Chapter 11

So I had to spend the rest of my life sitting in the library trying to compose a paper on consideration that would satisfy the inconsiderate Mr. Lambert. And I was off the paper on top of that. Life was not exactly a bowl of cherries or a bed of roses.

When I was finally sprung at five o'clock that afternoon, I slumped my way dejectedly home. Judy was in the kitchen giggling over something on the kitchen table.

"Oh, there you are, Granny." She looked up and smiled as I came in the back door. "What kept you?"

I didn't want to reopen the whole can of worms right then, so I passed it off with, "I had to stay late to finish an assignment."

I walked over to see what was so amusing on the table. Staring up at me were half a dozen blown up shots of the twins — the ones I had taken on the weekend.

"Where did these come from?" I asked in surprise.

"I found them in your father's den when I

was looking for the bank statement. I have no idea when he took them. Aren't they a hoot?"

"You like them?" I asked, even more surprised.

"They're great. Especially this one of Trixie bending over in the sandbox. Your father really is a marvellous candid photographer, Granny."

I cleared my throat and ventured a weak, "Ah, Judy, Dad didn't take those. I did. When you guys were in Seattle."

She looked up at me in amazement. "You? Why, Granny, I had no idea you were getting so good. If it's okay with you I'm going to have these framed and put them up in the rec room."

My heart jumped. "Sure, I don't mind." With just a few words she made me feel better than I had all day about my love affair with photography. At least someone liked my candid work.

"So how about the pictures that new photographer took of the girls? Have you got the new proofs back yet?" I asked, feeling a little embarrassed and wanting to change the subject.

"Yes, they came this morning." She jumped up from the table and started for the hall. "I'll get them for you to look at; they're just great." She was back in a minute with a large orange envelope which she opened, handing me the contents. "See for yourself."

I riffled through the proofs and sighed inwardly. They were the usual posed shots of the twins looking like a pair of Barbie dolls in their make-up, freshly set hair, and frilly dresses. They made Trina and Trixie look like beautiful children, but not real ones.

"Very nice," I murmured as I handed the pictures back to Judy and tried to look impressed. "What are you going to do with them?"

"As soon as we pick out the best ones and get them finished, I'm going to send them to the Tiny Tammy Toddler's Togs company. They're looking for a little girl to be Tiny Tammy in their new promotion. Just think how much more effective two Tiny Tammys would be." Her eyes lost focus as she went into her favourite vision of the twins taking the world by storm. I took advantage of her dream state to slip out of the kitchen and up to my room.

I just couldn't figure Judy out. She obviously recognized the appeal of my candid photos of the twins or she wouldn't have been so pleased with them. Yet they'd been replaced on the table in front of her within minutes by those artificial studio shots. If only she would recognize how hopeless her effort to get the twins launched was as long as she used awful photos like those.

§   §   §

The next day I was stuck at school until five o'clock again. But at least by the time I left I'd managed to write nearly three hundred words on consideration. And I was pretty sure they would please Mr. Lambert — they made me want to throw up!

I got home just in time for dinner, and found that Dad was back.

"So," he said as he sharpened the carving knife and studied the roast in front of him, "what's everyone been up to while I was gone?"

The twins, of course, got their word in first. Dad listened with apparent concentration to their complicated recital of games played, arguments fought, and TV shows watched over the last few days.

Then it was Judy's turn. She launched into a detailed account of the success of the latest proofs, the difficulty of choosing the best among them, and the length of time she would have to wait for the finished photos before she could send them in to the kid's clothing company contest she was going to enter.

"I hope I chose the right ones to finish. They were all so good," she beamed. "I just feel it in my bones that this time we're going to win."

"What did you say the name of the company was?" Dad asked as he helped himself to seconds of everything.

"Tiny Tammy Toddler's Togs," she replied.

"Hmm. They're based in Halifax, aren't they?"

"That's right. How did you know?"

"Oh, I don't know," he sounded vague. "I guess I must have read about them somewhere or seen an ad on TV. That name rather stands out in my mind." Then he turned to me and hurriedly changed the subject.

"How about you, Granny? Anything exciting happen while I was gone?"

So I gave him an extremely edited version of the last few days. I'd save the part about having to leave the paper for later — when no one else was around to witness my shame.

Dad listened to my dull account of schoolday routine with no sign that he noticed anything wrong, then got up from the table.

"Excuse me. I'll be back in a sec; don't anyone move."

Judy and I looked at each other questioningly, while the twins cried out in unison, "Presents!"

They were right. Dad returned with four packages and a smug grin. "Here we are," he said, handing me the first brightly wrapped parcel. "Hope you like it."

I love presents and surprises, and I knew from years of experience just how great Dad's could be. The parcel was about the size of a box of crackers, only much heavier. I tore off the paper, opened the box, and gasped. Inside was a compact little Nikon, a model similar to the one I had been using only newer. And tucked on either side were a 24mm wide-angle lens and an 80mm telephoto.

I jumped up and ran over to throw my arms around him. "Oh, Dad, it's beautiful! My very own camera!"

I suppose it seems strange that I should be so excited about being given a camera. After all, Dad had at least six that I was welcome to use whenever they were available. But it wasn't the same as having my own. For one thing, I wouldn't have to shoot a whole roll of film at a time so that the camera would be free when Dad wanted to use it. I could shoot at my own pace, when and if I felt like it. I could hardly wait to try it.

I was checking out the instruction manual when I noticed the excited chatter had suddenly stopped. I looked up and saw the twins staring in ecstacy at a couple of boxes full of model railway equipment. Judy was staring in disbelief.

"Gordon, do you really think that's a suitable present for the girls? It just seems . . . masculine."

"Nonsense," he told her firmly. "They're going to love it. Just look at their faces. This isn't the first time I've bought a railway for a little girl, you know."

"That's right, Judy," I chimed in. "Dad gave me a model railway when I was about the twins' age too. It was my favourite toy for years."

The twins were paying absolutely no attention to this exchange. They had opened up the boxes and were pulling out pieces and scattering them everywhere in their excitement.

"Remember, Dad, how you and Mom and I

would spend hours running it around the playroom?" I started to smile, then realized what a tactless thing that was to say. I glanced from Dad to Judy and opened my mouth to apologize, but Judy just caught my eye and shook her head with a small smile. Time to make a quiet getaway before I made things any worse, I decided.

"Come on, kids, let's take this stuff downstairs and I'll help you set it up."

The girls rushed to the door, dropping pieces of rail and plastic boxcars in their wake.

"Yes, you do that, Granny, thanks. And would you put them in bed later, please? Judy and I have some celebrating to do tonight. We're going out for a while."

"What's the occasion?" I asked.

"Our six-month anniversary."

As I left the room, I saw him hand the last package to Judy. Her happy "Oh, Gordon, it's just beautiful!" followed me down the stairs. Trust Dad to be able to make everyone happy in spite of my gaffe.

When he and Judy got home later that night, he came to my room to say goodnight.

"Now, Granny, let's hear the real story of the last few days," he said as soon as he came in the door.

I looked at him in amazement. How could he have known I was upset? The new camera he had brought me had taken a lot of the sting out of being off the paper, but it still hurt. I had been moping since the twins went to bed, but he couldn't have known that. Anyway, it sure felt good to get the whole story off my chest at last.

"Don't feel too bad, honey," he tried to comfort me when I stopped talking. "The world is full of people like those teachers, people who are so concerned about their image that they lose all sense of perspective. You just have to learn to feel sorry for them."

"But I wanted so much to be on the paper," I sighed.

"I know you did. And I guess it's partly my fault that you've had this trouble. I should have warned you that your teachers might take exception to those pictures. But they were so good, I'm afraid I just didn't think of what the consequences might be. Never mind though. You may be off the paper, but no one can stop you from being a photographer. And maybe in time your principal will reconsider and let you back on the *Speaker*."

"Not much chance of that. It would take a miracle," I muttered.

"Well, you never know. Miracles have been known to happen."

I smiled faintly and nodded my head once in agreement. But I knew in my heart he was being completely unrealistic.

Chapter 12

You won't believe what happened next — I got back on the paper!

It happened after school the next day when I turned in my masterpiece on consideration to Mr. Lambert. I'd finished it during study period, and as soon as the last bell rang I took it to the office. I tried giving it to the secretary to pass on, but she wasn't having any of that.

"Mr. Lambert asked me to send you right in, Granny." I guess my expression must have spelled sheer panic, because she laughed and said, "Don't worry, I think it might be good news."

I could use a little of that, but I didn't hold out a lot of hope.

"Ah, Granada," Mr. Lambert greeted me, standing and smiling like I was a real person and not just a student. "Come in, come in. Take a seat."

I looked nervously at him, then slipped into the chair once occupied by Ms. Hackett and waited for the axe to fall.

"I see you've finished your essay. Good for

you, although it wasn't really necessary." He reached over and took the loose-leaf pages from my hand, glanced casually at them, and tossed them on his desk.

He beamed again, and I wondered if something had made him go a little funny over the past few days. Amnesia came quickly to mind.

"I've just been informed that your father is Gordon Tyler."

I confessed that it was true, although I couldn't see what the big revelation was. After all, that stuff was in my file.

"That certainly explains your unusual photographic contribution to the paper," Mr Lambert was continuing. "I assure you, if I had known you were the daughter of such a well-known photojournalist I would have understood why you did what you did. No doubt your father has passed his considerable talents on to you."

For once in my life I kept my mouth shut and waited to see what would happen next.

"In view of the fact that you were practising your profession," he lifted his eyebrows significantly, "rather than trying to make your teachers look foolish as I originally assumed, I see no reason why you should not continue on the *Speaker*."

It took a minute for his words to sink in, and when they did I jumped up and cried, "Gee whillikers! That's really keen!" Under emotional stress I tend to forget Maureen's training.

He continued to beam at me while I got myself under control.

"Thank you very much, Mr. Lambert," I finally said. "I assure you I won't take any more photos that might cause anyone embarrassment."

"I'm sure you won't, my dear."

I smiled and practically ran out of the room before he could change his mind.

Maureen was waiting for me at the bike racks. I couldn't wait to tell her the good news.

"I don't understand why he suddenly decided that Gordon Tyler's little girl could do no wrong. He must have known who I was when I registered." I got on my bike and peddled across the grounds to the street.

"Probably he didn't associate you with the famous photographer," Maureen answered from behind. "After all, Tyler isn't that uncommon a name."

"But why now?" I asked. She didn't have an answer, and we rode in silence until we came to her house. We flopped into the wicker chairs on her front porch and I continued to puzzle over the problem.

"Want some lemonade?" Maureen started to get up.

"Steve!"

"Where?"

"No, Steve must have told Mr. Lambert about Dad. He probably convinced him that it was a real coup getting the daughter of a big-time photographer on the paper." I sat up and hugged my knees. "Boy, if he only knew the truth about what a rank amateur I am."

"Do you really think Steve would do that? It doesn't sound like him."

"Of course it was him. Who else?" I jumped up and ran down the stairs.

"Hey, where are you going? Don't you want that lemonade?"

"I'll take a raincheck. I'm going back to the school to try and catch Steve before he leaves. He might still be in his office. I've just got to tell him the good news and thank him for what he did." I picked up my bike, waved, and was off down the street before she could get her mouth closed.

Steve was in the office when I burst in a few minutes later. He and Lonnie Kaye were on the old couch that sits behind the layout table going at it hot and heavy.

"Oh, I'm terribly sorry," I mumbled as they came up for air and glared at me. That is, Lonnie glared; Steve just looked sheepish.

"As usual, your timing is marvellous, Granada," Lonnie sighed. Then, as she sat up and began straightening her clothes, she gave me a puzzled look. "Hey, I thought you were kicked off the paper."

I decided to ignore her and turned to Steve.

"That's what I came to tell you. Lambert has

reinstated me. I'm back on the paper!"

"Whoopdedoo," Lonnie muttered, getting up from the couch.

Steve was much more enthusiastic. "You're back on the paper? That's great." He stood up and walked over to where I was leaning against the door jam. "What made him change his mind?"

"As if you didn't know," I grinned. "Thanks a lot, Steve."

He looked baffled for a moment, then grinned back. "Sure, Granny, any time."

"I'm sorry about barging in, but I couldn't wait to tell you the news. I'll be getting along now." I suddenly felt very embarrassed, thinking about what I had just interrupted.

"Yeah, well, okay." He looked over to where Lonnie was standing, tapping her foot and shooting daggers. "See you tomorrow after school. Friday is planning day, remember?"

I remembered. It seemed like a year had passed since the last planning day two weeks ago.

"I'll be there," I smiled.

"I just bet you will. Why don't you —" I left before Lonnie could finish her sarcastic suggestion.

As I rounded the corner after I had retrieved my bike, I was delighted to see Steve and Lonnie climbing into his car and driving off. Not that I was so pleased that he was with Lonnie, but I was a lot happier knowing that they were in the car instead of on the couch.

§   §   §

"Granny, did you see a pile of photos on the desk in the studio?" Dad's voice called from downstairs. I was on the phone bringing Maureen up to date on what had happened after I left her standing on her porch with our lemonade.

"Just a sec, I'll be right back." I laid the phone down and went into the hall. "No, I haven't even been in the studio for a few days. What were they?"

"Those blow-ups I did of the shots you took of the twins. I thought that's where I put them, but I can't find them anywhere. Well, never mind. I'll just have to redo them."

"Hey, wait," I cried and started for the stairs. "Judy has the —" But he was already gone .

I shrugged and went back into my room. I could tell him about Judy having the pictures framed later, but right now Maureen was waiting impatiently on the phone.

"So anyway, I'm going to the staff planning meeting tomorrow after school," I continued. "Boy, I can't wait to see Gary O'Hare's face when he sees me there. He'll be destroyed!"

"Don't be so sure, Granny. Toby told me that Gary said he thinks your work is technically very good. It was the subject matter of those three pictures that he objected to."

"I suppose he would say that under the circumstances. Steve probably told him he'd talked to Lambert and that I'd likely be back on the paper. He's just covering his tracks."

"Well, maybe," she answered doubtfully. Then she changed the subject. "Are you going to the Fall Fling, Granny?"

The Fall Fling is the first major social event of the school year. It's a dance, of course, held in the auditorium and attended by freshmen, sophomores, juniors and seniors. It was going to be on Hallowe'en night, which was still a long way off, but apparently everyone started planning for school activities like that way ahead of time.

"No one's asked me, Maureen," I answered.

"Oh, don't worry about that, someone will. There's lots of time yet. And if no one does, I can always get Toby to fix you up with one of his friends."

"Come on, Maureen. I'd rather catch bubonic plague than get 'fixed up' with a total stranger."

"That's dumb. All kinds of guys would love to date you if they knew you. Anyway, there's lots of time to work something out."

"We'll see. Maybe by the time the dance rolls around Steve and Lonnie will have broken up."

"Don't hold your breath," she advised.

I hung up and laid back on the bed. Maybe Steve and Lonnie would break up in spite of

Maureen's pessimism. Steve seemed to like me quite a bit, and I could just keep building on that. Or so I hoped. I started on a long involved daydream about Lonnie losing her hair and developing an acute case of acne.

An hour or so later I reluctantly got up and began my homework. Dad and the photos never crossed my mind again.

Chapter 13

The next three weeks turned out to be pretty amazing. Among other things, I became completely at home with the darkroom and my beautiful new camera, we put out two editions of the paper, both with a number of my photos, and Gary O'Hare turned out to be human.

The October 7th edition of the *Speaker* featured extra-curricular activities. Gary assigned me drama and basketball, and I got a number of shots that he deigned to admit were printable. The next edition was on volunteer work, and I managed to shoot some stuff at a nursing home that he printed. Of course, he never complimented me directly, but he did make some nice comments to Steve about my work, and Steve passed them on to me.

I managed to wangle a total of two Coke dates with Steve during those three weeks. Both times we went to some out-of-the-way spot where no one from the school was likely to see us and spent the whole time discussing my work and the *Speaker* in general. I wasn't crazy about the arrangement, but I was willing to put up with it just to be with Steve. I was still optimistic that he would dump Lonnie, and I figured things would get better then.

Lonnie, of course, continued to be poisonous toward me. She couldn't have known anything about my dates with Steve though, so she was just being poisonous on general principles. Well, no, that's not quite true. There was the little matter of the basketball team.

She and I had both made first string forward, which practically guaranteed that our team would finish last in the league, until Ms Hackett realized that Lonnie was refusing to pass to me and demoted her to second string. Needless to say, that didn't help our relationship.

Away from school, things continued much as usual. Judy sent off the studio portraits of the twins to the Tiny Tammy contest, then began practically living beside the mailbox. She was still sure they would win, and I was equally sure they didn't have a chance, unless Mr. Tiny Tammy was planning a campaign featuring zombies. To avoid trouble, I carefully avoided any conversation that might bring up the subject.

Dad had to go away again for two weeks, this time to China to do a feature on Barefoot Doctors. That was a really terrific program that took certain people from remote villages into the city to get basic medical training, kind of like our paramedics. Then they went back to their villages and continued in their regular jobs, but were available to provide simple medical treatment when needed. I had pretty well decided that's what I would do when I finished school. No, not be a Barefoot Doctor, be a photojournalist like Dad.

Around the middle of October, Maureen actually landed the lead in the Christmas play. That was enough to start her walking around in a totally different space from the rest of us. Whenever I wasn't out somewhere with my camera, I found myself sitting in her bedroom cuing her lines for her. The play wouldn't open until mid-December, and then only for three nights, but Maureen was treating it like a Broadway opening. There was no doubt about it, she would be dynamite

She did take enough time out of her practice session one day to let me know what she thought of my brain though. A couple of guys in my year had asked me to the Fall Fling, but I turned them both down. There wasn't anything wrong with them; it was just that I kept hoping maybe Steve would ask me and I wanted to be free.

When I told Maureen what had happened her jaw and her copy of the script both dropped.

"Granny, you're ruining your life," she announced. "You're going to end up not going to the dance at all, you know."

Of course, that was my worst fear, but I

wasn't about to admit that to her. So I just assured her that Steve was going to ask me any day now and that I refused to settle for anything less than him.

But the look she gave me was full of pity as she returned to the lines in front of her. And by the Friday before the dance I began to wish that I had listened to her. By then Lonnie Kaye had made sure everyone knew she was giong to the dance with Steve, and I hadn't received any more invitations. So I was in a lousy mood when I walked into the usual bi-weekly planning session for the paper that night.

The dance was the main subject of discussion. Everyone agreed that it should be tha main theme of the next paper, which would be coming out just four days later. Steve wanted a double page photographic spread of candid shots to go with the write-up. I expected Gary to take the assignment himself and leave me the thrilling job of covering the chess tournament that was being held the same weekend. It looked like I wouldn't even get a look at the Fall Fling.

You can imagine how completely stunned I was when Gary caught me after the meeting and said, "Granola, I guess you'll have to cover the dance."

"Granada," I growled. Then I suddenly realized what he had said and looked up in amazement. "You mean you want me to do it? All by myself?"

"That's the general idea. If you don't think you're up to it I'll see if Toby can help out. He's not great, but he does know a lens from a light metre."

"Of course I can handle it," I shot back. "But how come you're not taking such a fantastic assignment for yourself?"

Anger and something that looked a lot like hurt crossed his face. "There's no way I can be in the band and on the floor at the same time," he said shortly. "I would have thought you could figure that out for yourself."

I had completely forgotten that Gary played drums in the school orchestra. I'd heard him a couple of times and had to admit he was very good, but not to him of course! He probably knew that better than anyone else anyway.

"What kind of shots do you want me to get?" I asked in a quiet voice. I was so elated about having an excuse to go to the dance legitimately on my own that I refused to let his patronizing get to me. I would not fight with him.

"The usual," he answered. "Kids dancing, the chaperones, anything funny or unusual you might catch. But please, Granada, nothing we'd get in trouble printing, okay?"

He still hadn't forgotten about the fiasco with the spread on the teachers. And apparently he wasn't about to let me forget either.

"I'm sure I can take a few pictures that would meet even your approval," I smiled sweetly and bit hard on my tongue. I turned to leave the room, but he called me back.

"Hey, wait a minute. We're going to have a problem with the timing. The dance is on Friday, which is the day we're supposed to have our copy in to the printer, but Steve's managed to get an extension till two o'clock Saturday. You'll have to have your stuff developed and into the office Saturday morning so I have time to look it over. Is that too much of a hassle? If so, I can develop it for you."

For a fleeting moment I thought I detected a flicker of friendliness in his face. Was he actually being nice to me after all these weeks?

"No problem," I answered. "I'll do the developing at home and have the prints to you by twelve o'clock at the latest."

At my words a scowl replaced the friendly look on his face.

"Oh, that's right, I forgot for a minute. Daddy develops your pictures for you?"

"He does not! I do all my own work!"

"Come on, Granada, remember I've seen you operating in the darkroom here. You don't know the first thing about it. The photos you've been handing in lately are very good, but you and I both know it's because you have a resident professional to make your stuff look great."

"That's not true," I protested. "Sure, I'll admit my Dad's taught me everything I know, but he doesn't do my work for me."

Gary looked uncertain and didn't answer for a minute. Then he said grudgingly, "Well, if that's true you've sure come a long way in a very short time. Maybe I've underestimated you."

"Maybe you have." I glared at him.

"On the other hand, you did screw up royally with those shots you took of the teachers." He glared back.

"You're just jealous because your photos were so dull. Besides, Steve thought mine were great, and he managed to convince Mr. Lambert they were okay too." I tossed my red head.

"Me jealous? Dull? Steve? What are you talking about?" He tossed his red head.

We glared at each other some more. Then Gary dropped his eyes and turned away. "If that's what you want to think, Granny, be my guest," he said, his voice soft and sad. He walked back over to his desk.

"What else am I supposed to think?" I shouted after him. "You were the one who told Lambert I was the one who took those pictures. I suppose I shouldn't blame you, but —"

He spun around and shouted back, "I didn't tell Lambert any such thing. As a matter of fact, I insisted that both our names be under all the photos so if there was any trouble you wouldn't have to take all the blame."

My mouth dropped open and I stared at him. "You didn't tell him? Then how did he know?"

"The whole school knew, Granny. Maureen

went to a lot of trouble to make sure of that."

I thought for a minute. "Well, maybe that's true," I said at last. "But admit it, you were delighted when I was kicked off the paper."

"What gave you that idea?"

"Oh, the way you practically did handstands when you heard the news. And you weren't exactly joyful when Steve got me reinstated."

"Did Steve tell you that? That he got you reinstated, I mean?"

I thought back for a minute. "No, not in so many words. But someone went to Lambert on my behalf. Who else but Steve?"

He didn't say anything, just looked at me with that same half-sad expression he had had when he told me to think what I liked.

It took me another whole minute to finally catch on, but please remember, I'm just not used to these North American intrigues.

"You mean it was you who talked Lambert into letting me come back on the paper?"

He shrugged his shoulders and looked down at his sneakers.

"But why? I thought you hated me?"

"I did at first, when you came on so phony. But later you looked like you were really trying, and I knew the photos you were handing in had to be yours. I admit I thought your dad had worked on your negs, but still they had to be good to start with."

"Honestly Gary, I don't know what to say.

I'm sorry I misjudged you.

I told you I always lose control of my tongue when I'm under emotional stress.

His face turned as red as mine and he shrugged again. "I did it for the paper," he said. "You're a good photographer, and the *Speaker* needs you. I'll be gone next year, and there isn't anyone else as good as you to take over my job."

I was pleased at the compliment, but a little hurt that his reason for helping me was strictly business. Still, it didn't really matter that much. I certainly had no romantic interest in him.

"Well, thanks again." I started out the door. "I'll see you Monday, I guess."

"Yeah, sure. Monday." He gave me a funny look and went into the darkroom. So — Gary O'Hare was not all bad. Would wonders never cease?

Chapter 14

The next day was another memorable one at the Tyler residence.

It started in the morning, when Judy finally got her letter from the Tiny Tammy company. Actually, the letter had been sitting in the mailbox since the day before, because Judy had been seized by an attack of nerves and refused to bring in the day's mail. But when I got back from my Saturday morning jogging session, I decided enough was enough and pulled the bundle of letters out of the mailbox and took them into the kitchen, where everyone was eating. I flopped down in my chair and started sorting through them.

"Here's a letter for you, Judy." I tossed the envelope casually onto the table and reached for my orange juice while I waited to see her reaction.

"Granny, aren't you going to wash up before — letter? Quick, give it to me!"

I shoved it closer to her, then handed Dad a fistful of bills and started to open a letter from my former Swiss roommate.

I hadn't even managed to get it halfway open when Judy screamed, "It's from the Tody Timmy Tagglers' Tons people!"

I grinned. "The who?"

"The Tommy Taggy Tiddlers' — Oh, never mind. Please, somebody open it for me. I'm all thumbs."

Dad took the letter from her and slit it open with his butter knife.

"Go ahead, you read it. I'm too nervous."

He glanced quickly over the contents, frowned and muttered, "That's odd."

"For goodness sake, Gordon, what does it say?" Judy was gulping shallow breaths and turning pink.

He shook his head in confusion and began to read:

Dear Mrs. Tyler:

This letter is to inform you that the six finalists have been chosen in our Tiny Tammy Toddler's Togs contest. The decision was very difficult to make as we had so many excellent entries. However, I am sorry to report that your child was not one of the winners.

May I wish you future success in finding a suitable modelling opportunity for your little girl.

Sincerely,

Carl Tomasa, President
Tiny Tammy Toddler's Togs Ltd.

I glanced over at Judy and felt like crying. She looked like she had just won Super Lotto but the ticket had been burned. She reached for the letter and began to reread it. I guess she hoped maybe Dad had forgotten how to decipher words.

"Listen to this," she cried. "Your child. They didn't even know I had entered twins. The models were probably picked before the contest was even advertised. I bet they didn't even look at the twins' photos."

"Does that mean we won't be on television?" Trixie looked hopeful.

Judy gave her a sad smile. "I'm afraid so, darling. But there are lots more contests. We'll win the next one, just you wait and see."

"Do we have to enter another contest?" That was Trina.

Judy stared at her daughters in amazement. "Well, of course we do," she said finally. "How else are you girls going to become known? Don't worry, you'll soon be having so much fun modelling that you'll forget how discouraging these contests can be."

But the twins' questions bothered me. It was obvious that both girls were uninterested in Judy's ambitions. If they had their way, they would spend the rest of their lives in the play room crashing trains into papier-mâché mountains.

So that was the morning.

In the afternoon I went over to Maureen's to help her with her lines again. I really didn't think she needed me, she was letter perfect already. But I went anyway. When I rang the doorbell, I could hear Rambo barking his head off and throwing himself against the door. Maureen let me in, keeping herself between me and her wild animal. Rambo, I should tell you, is a five-pound toy poodle. He spends the majority of his days trying to live up to his name, and his doting family goes along with the gag.

We went directly to her room in the basement and took our customary play rehearsal positions: me on the bed, Maureen on the floor, Rambo guarding the door. But instead of pulling out the dog-eared script, Maureen settled back against the floor cushions and announced, "I've got a surprise for you."

I was a little suspicious of the smug look on her face. The last time she had a surprise for me, I spent an entire Sunday afternoon in a converted factory watching two bad actors wait for Godot.

"So? What's the surprise?"

"Granny, how many dates have you had since you started at Fi High?"

"Three," I answered promptly. The number was engraved on my brain.

"And all Coke dates with Steve Williams, right?"

"Of course."

"Well, I think that's unhealthy. All kinds of guys would like to date you, but you might as well be living in a cloister except for those clandestine meetings with Steve. So I've decided to do something about it."

Oh, God! It was worse than I thought.

"Toby and I are going to see the *Prospect Pointers* tonight at the Q.E. I asked Toby to get a date for you so we could double."

"Morrie, you didn't!"

"Sure I did. If *you* won't do something about your social life, then I'm going to." She held up her hand as I started to climb off the bed. "Don't try to get out of it," she warned me. "It's all settled. Toby and your date are coming here first, then we'll all come and pick you up."

I stared at her for a minute, then realized there was no point in arguing. Besides, she was right in a way. I *was* missing out on a lot of fun while I waited for Steve to see the error of his ways and dump Lonnie Kaye.

"So who's the guy?" I asked, suspecting it probably wasn't someone from any of my classes since Toby was a senior.

"That's the second part of the surprise," she grinned. "You'll have to wait to find out. Just be ready to go a little before eight. And wear something more formal than your jogging suit, eh? This is a *tony* place we're going to." She sat up and reached for the script on the dressing table beside her. "Now, on to work. I want to get your opinion of this new idea I have for playing the second scene in act three."

So that was the afternoon.

When I got home a little after five, Trixie and Trina met me at the door gabbling in unintelligible unison. The only words I was able to sort out were "airplane" and "trip." I walked into the dining room and found Judy and Dad pouring over a bunch of lists.

"Hey, what's up?" I asked, dropping into a seat across from them. "What are the girls talking about?"

Judy stopped writing furiously and looked up at me with an angelic smile.

"Granny, you'll never guess what happened."

No, I probably wouldn't. But at a guess I'd say it probably had something to do with travelling.

"The Tiny Tammy P.R. man called just after you left. The girls made the finals in the contest after all!"

"But what about that letter you got this morning?"

"I guess there was some sort of mix-up. Anyway, it doesn't matter. The important thing is that the girls were chosen. We have to be in Halifax next Monday for the interviews with the panel that will pick the winner."

"And the twins have decided they want to be in the contest after all if it means they get a trip in an airplane, right? That's terrific, Judy." I meant it too. The contest was so important to her, and apparently I had overestimated how much the girls disliked modelling.

But I still couldn't understand how anyone could have been impressed with those phony pictures of the girls Judy had sent in. "I guess your new photographer must have known more..." I let my voice die out as I saw Dad frantically signalling me to shut up. He stood up and motioned for me to follow him into his den. I don't think Judy even knew we'd left the room.

"What was *that* all about," I demanded as I took a chair beside him.

"It's the pictures, sweetie. Don't mention them in front of Judy."

"Why, for heaven's sake?"

He looked embarrassed and cleared his throat. "Well, it's this way. Remember those candid shots you took of the girls a few weeks ago?"

I nodded.

"Well, you may recall I asked you if I could blow up some of them."

"Yeah, but Judy found those and took them to be framed."

"So that's what happened to them, eh?" he grinned. "Well, I still had the negs, so I did up another batch and sent them to my friend, Carl Tomasa, at Tiny Tammy's. I thought he might be interested in using a couple of them for advertising. What I *didn't* expect was that he would consider them for the contest he's promoting. Anyway, when I got home from China I gave him a call to see if he'd received the pictures. He said he had and that the girls were in the finals. That's why I was so surprised when Judy got that letter this morning."

"So then what?"

"Well, I put in another call to Carl to find out what had happened. It turns out that the letter was sent to Judy based on those photos she had taken by that guy downtown. The finalists were notified by telegram, but in our case it was addressed to me at my office at the paper instead of here. It's probably been chasing me all around the Orient."

"Oh, my golly! So Judy thinks those dreadful photos she sent won."

"You've got it. And given the circumstances, I think it's best she goes on believing just that. I don't want her feeling bad."

I started to laugh. "Dad, do you realize what this means? No, I'm not referring to Judy and twins — that's wonderful, I guess. But it means that my photographs were good enough to get the girls into the finals."

"Of course they were good enough. You've got a natural talent that can't be learned, Granny. You could be great some day if you stick with it."

If he'd told me I had just won the Nobel

Peace Prize I couldn't have been prouder.

"Now," he rose up and reached for my hand, "we'd better get back to the circus before Judy notices we're not listening to her. Remember now, not a word about the photos. This is our little secret."

"Got it." I stood up and grinned. "What do you think will happen when the judges get a load of the twins in their pink tulle and blue eye shadow?"

He shuddered and opened the door. "We'll just have to try to persuade Judy to play down the Barbie doll image a little. You try talking to her, Granny."

Before I could protest that I had about as much chance of influencing Judy as I had of ordering rain to fall, he was out the door and down the hall.

Chapter 15

After all the excitement of the day, I was almost dreading what the evening would bring. Luckily, dinner was take-out Chinese. No preparation and clean-up meant I could use every available minute to prepare myself.

Not that I was planning any major changes in my appearance; what I needed was time to psych myself up for my very first real Canadian high school type date. I had gone out with boys while I was in school in Europe, but that was quite a different thing. Mostly my dates were brothers of classmates or sons of my father's friends. And always they were European boys: French, Italian, German. I'd never dated a North American boy in my entire life. I was mildly terrified.

When the doorbell rang at ten-to-eight I had already showered, tamed my hair, and climbed into a grey flannel skirt and pale blue angora sweater. I rubbed a little blusher on my cheeks, ran a gloss over my lips, and partially hid the freckles on my nose with a make-up base. The doorbell ran a second time. I took one final look in the full-length mirror, mentally cursed my dear departed Grandmother Tyler for passing on her pale red eyebrows and lashes to me, and ran down the stairs to meet my fate.

I threw open the door.

"You!" I cried.

"You!" Gary O'Hare answered.

"What are you doing here?"

"I came to pick up my blind date. What are *you* doing here?"

"I live here."

"Then you're. . ."

"I guess."

Neither of us could seem to think of anything to add to this sparkling exchange. We just stood there staring at each other for what seemed like another day or so. Finally Dad's voice behind me brought us out of our mutual trance.

"Bring the young man in, Granny, and let us meet him."

I stepped aside and motioned for Gary to come into the hall.

"Hello, there." Dad walked over and put out his hand. "I'm Gordon Tyler, Granny's father."

Gary's mouth dropped open and he stood there gaping in complete awe. Finally he reached out and took his hand. "It's an honour to meet you, sir. I'm Gary O'Hare, one of your greatest fans." He shuffled and turned bright pink.

"Oh, really? That's very flattering. Are you a photographer too, Gary?" he asked as he moved toward the living room with Gary practically stuck to his right side.

"I'm just an amateur, sir, but I'm thinking about majoring in journalism with an emphasis on photography when I go to college next year."

"Wonderful." Dad sat down and for a moment I thought Gary was going to kneel in front of him. Instead, he dropped down on a stool and settled for just gazing adoringly up at him.

"This is my wife, Judy." Dad gestured to where she was sitting across the room, trying to keep a straight face. Not that it would have mattered if she'd suddenly jumped up and started stripping. Gary didn't take his eyes off Dad.

"Maybe you could show me some of your work some time," Dad continued, his eyes full of laughter. "What kind of camera do you use?"

"The school has an old Leica that I use for most of the stuff for the paper. My own camera is a Konika."

"A Leica, you say? That's great. My first. . ."

The doorbell rang again, and I left my post at the doorway to answer it.

"Hey, what's holding you guys up?" Maureen asked, peering around me into the hall. "Where's Gary?"

"Maureen! What did you think you were doing?"

"Oh, you mean your blind date. I told you you would be surprised. What happened to him anyway?"

"He's in the living room worshiping my father. I think he'd rather date him than me."

A horn honked impatiently from the car sitting in front of the house.

"Come on," Maureen grabbed me by the hand and dragged me back to the living room. "We're going to be late if we don't leave right away."

Dad got up when he saw Maureen standing in the entranceway. "Oh, I'm sorry, girls. I'm afraid I've been keeping this young man." He smiled sheepishly at us, then turned back to Gary. "Perhaps you can come over again and bring a few samples of your work. I'd like you to see the new enlarger I bought when I was in Japan a few months ago. It's totally computerized."

"Hey, that's awesome."

Maureen and I began walking toward the front door, and Gary reluctantly tore himself away from Dad and followed us, glancing longingly back to the living room. I pushed the door open and marched toward the car, cursing the time I had taken to dress up for my big date. I could have been wearing a grass skirt and tassels and I don't think Gary would have even noticed.

The twenty-minute ride downtown was

charged with all kinds of conflicting vibes. Gary was still radiating from his encounter with the great Gordon Tyler. I was numb with anger both at Gary for ignoring me and at Maureen for setting up this ridiculous party. Maureen, sensing that all was not going smoothly in the back seat, was anxious, and Toby was upset about being late for the concert. Nobody said anything until we got to the Q.E. auditorium, and then Toby only muttered, "You guys get out here; I'll find a place to park and meet you inside."

The place was a seething mass of teenage bodies all screaming at the top of their lungs. A peculiar pungent odour hit us the minute we walked in the door. Before I could embarrass myself by asking what the smell was, Toby rejoined us. "Geez, smell that pot. Looks like half the audience is stoned already."

We went through the inner doors and found our seats after stumbling over a comatose body sprawled in the aisle. I began to wonder what horror film I'd wandered into.

Maureen went down the row first, followed by Toby. Gary motioned me to go in next, then took the aisle seat beside me. I was saved from having to find something to say to him when the curtain on stage opened and a man in a tuxedo stepped forward. He held up his hand for silence and was greeted by more yells and catcalls. He made a futile attempt to get the crowd's attention, then gave up and left the stage. A moment later six young men dressed in long grey robes, each sporting a different pastel-coloured head of hair, galloped onto the stage. The decibel level around me rose another thousand or so points, and my head started to leave my body.

Finally the crowd quieted down and the group began playing and singing. At least, I *think* that's what they were doing. I'd never heard hard rock live before and was completely unprepared for the impact it had on my central nervous system. I honestly didn't know how I was going to sit through the next two hours.

I shifted my eyes casually over to my three companions. Maureen was glowing, Toby was standing up yelling with the rest of the crowd, Gary was looking bored. He caught me watching him and tried to smile, but it didn't really come off. I couldn't tell whether it was the concert or me that was putting him off, and at that point I didn't really care.

When the band finished its first number, the crowd went into another frenzy of uncontrolled hysteria. My head was sending loud warning messages to my brain and my stomach suddenly contracted. It was pretty obvious I was going to have to do something before I either passed out or threw up. I gripped the arm rests and took a couple of deep breaths as the music started again.

"Hey, are you okay?" Gary was leaning over me looking downright concerned.

"It — it's the noise. I'm sorry. I'm just not used to —" My stomach gave another rumble and I jumped up from my seat. "Excuse me. I've got to —" I pushed past Gary and ran up the aisle.

I made it to the ladies' room just in time. Charlie Wong's wonderful egg rolls followed the ginger beef and fried rice right in front of me. When I was finally through, I leaned back against the door exhausted. As the muted sounds of the Prospect Pointers and their frantic fans seeped through the walls, I wondered how long I could stay in my refuge before Maureen came looking for me. I was brought back to reality a few minutes later by a timid knock on the door and Gary's voice calling, "Hey, are you okay in there?"

I stood up, flushed the toilet, and went out into the outer room. "I'm fine," I called back.

After splashing cold water on my face and rinsing my mouth out, I ran a comb through my damp hair. Then I mentally steeled myself for the confrontation with Gary, whom I was sure would be completely fed up with me by now.

"God, Granny, you look awful!" were Gary's encouraging words of greeting as I came through the door.

"I'm sorry. I guess the noise and the atmosphere . . . Look, why don't you go back? I'll just stay out here for a while till I feel a little better. I don't want you to miss the concert."

"Me miss the concert? Don't I wish. But it's you who'll really miss it. Maureen told me what a big fan you are of the Prospects, but she didn't actually tell me it was you. Just that my blind date loved hard rock."

I started to laugh in spite of everything. "Gary, I don't think I've ever enjoyed anything less than that little taste of hard rock, thank you very much. I guess Maureen was trying to make me look like I was really with it. She thinks I'm a relic of the Stone Age."

He looked completely confused, then began to laugh with me. "What are we waiting for then? Let's get out of this place. I'll run back and tell them we're leaving. We can meet them here when the concert's over."

Fifteen minutes later Gary and I were sitting across from each other at a formica table in the Snoball Café.

"I want you to have some tea and dry toast while we're here. It's the best thing for an upset stomach," he informed me.

"Oh? And where did you study medicine?" I asked, a little amused at his authoritative attitude.

"My mother's a nurse," he answered, ignoring my sarcasm. "My Dad's a medic too, but he's better with heads than stomachs. He's a psychiatrist."

"I could have used him back there when the band went into their first number," I giggled. "I thought I was going to lose mine."

He laughed again and I suddenly realized that I'd never really seen him without his customary scowl before. He looked entirely different. Not great looking like Steve, but nice.

I began to relax. "And is that all of your family, or do you have brothers and sisters?"

"One of each, both younger than me. Sandy, my little sister, is just six and a pain in the butt. Buddy is three years older and idolizes me — smart little kid that he is." He grinned and asked, "What about you?"

"Two stepsisters. Terminally cute, but okay."

My tea and toast came, and I nibbled obediently on them while Gary started telling me about the latest stunt Sandy had pulled.

I was on my third pot of tea when Gary suddenly looked at his watch and exclaimed, "It's after eleven! The concert was probably over half an hour ago. Maureen and Toby will be going nuts."

He picked up the bill, looked at it, and threw some money on the counter. "Come on, Granny, we'd better get back to the Q.E. and hope they're still there waiting for us."

He helped me into my jacket, took my arm, and steered me possessively out the door.

Maureen and Toby were just leaving the concert hall as we reached it again and dove in to escape the pouring rain that had apparently started while we were in the café.

"Hey, there you are," Toby called. "We'd just about given up on you. Wait here, I'll get the car."

"Are you okay, Granny?" Maureen looked anxiously at me as we stood huddled under the canopy waiting for Toby.

"I'm fine now. I had a touch of indigestion, but I received excellent medical treatment and it's gone now."

Gary's laugh rang out beside me.

Maureen glared menacingly at him. "You mean you've been to the hospital? You should have told me, Granny. I'd have gone with you."

"No need, I was in excellent hands. Did you enjoy the concert?"

"Oh, it was tremendous. You don't know what you missed."

"I think I probably do, Morrie."

Before she could probe any further, Toby's car glided up to the curb. Gary took my arm and smiled down at me as he helped me into the back seat. Maureen watched us, her mouth gaping.

"On second thought," she muttered to herself, "I wonder if maybe I missed something."

Gary slid in beside me and took my hand. "Could be," he answered.

§   §   §

I had barely got my eyes open the next morning when the phone rang. Judy and Dad try to sleep in on Sundays, so I took the call on the extension in my bedroom. It was Maureen.

"Okay, tell me all," she demanded.

"All what?" I was still a little groggy and not thinking too clearly.

"You and Gary. It looked like you really hit it off last night."

The events of the evening before came gradually back into my conscious mind and I began to smile to myself.

"I guess you could say that. We talked for ages in that funny little cafe and really got to know each other. He's much nicer than he seemed at first."

"That's what I've been trying to tell you, Granny. So when is your next date?"

"Oh, no, Morrie. You've got it all wrong. Gary and I have resolved our differences, but we're just friends, nothing romantic. I'm saving that for Steve."

The only sound for the next thirty seconds was the hum on the telephone wire.

"I see," she said at last. "I think you're nuts, but it's your life, I guess. However, I don't think Gary sees things quite the way you do. The way he was looking at you last night was not buddy-buddy."

"No way," I laughed. "You're the one who's nuts, Morrie. Look, I have to go. I can hear rumblings from the rest of the household, and I want to get my jogging in before breakfast."

"Okay. Are you coming over later?"

"Sure. See you around two." I hung up and

began getting undressed.

I'd have to get Maureen straightened out on the status of Gary and me before she started trying to promote something. Lots of time to do it this afternoon though, or so I thought. But when I came in from my run an hour later, the first person I saw sitting at the breakfast table was Gary.

Chapter 16

"What are you doing here?" I burst out, Maureen's words on the telephone earlier still bright in my mind.

The smile that had started to cross Gary's face faded, and his regulation scowl replaced it.

"He called while you were jogging and I invited him over, Granny," Dad answered, frowning. Then he turned to Gary. "If you're ready we can get at it." He took a last gulp of coffee, wiped his mouth, and stood up. Gary followed suit. I sat down in the chair Gary had vacated and reached for the toast. We didn't look at each other.

Now before you get to thinking that maybe Maureen was right about Gary's interest in me, let me assure you it was Dad he came to see. They spent the whole morning closeted in the studio together. And it was the same when he came again on Tuesday and Thursday. I was away both days, but Dad reported on the visits.

"That young man is very talented," he announced Friday morning. "And so polite and cheerful. Too bad you missed him, Granny. He asked about you and seemed disappounted that you weren't home. Do I sense a more than passing interest in my best girl?"

I was still sure Gary's sudden interest in the Tyler household had little to do with me and a lot to do with photography, and I told Dad so in no uncertain terms. But I was pleased that Gary had asked about me. I still wanted to be friends with him and I realized how impolite I had been on Sunday morning. I hadn't seen him at school all week though — not to talk to anyway — so I hadn't had a chance to apologize. I was hoping I would finally get my chance at the Fall Fling that night.

If I made it to the dance, that is. There was a point when I seriously doubted that I would, I was so nervous. And guess who saved me. Judy.

She and the twins were leaving for Halifax the next day. Judy spent all of Friday running around getting the girls ready. She had their hair professionally permed and styled and bought them each three new outfits. I took every opportunity to suggest to her that she shouldn't try so hard to improve on nature, just let the girls be themselves. But she didn't exactly hang on my every word.

Finally, I gave up and went to my own room to get ready for the dance. I started frantically trying on everthing I owned, unable to decide what to wear. Even though I was going strictly on a working basis, I was determined to make

Steve notice me. But I had no idea what the occassion called for.

Maureen had been absolutely no help when I asked her. She was planning to wear an orange sari her mother had brought her from India last year, even though this wasn't supposed to be the usual Hallowe'en dress-up affair. But then, no one expected Maureen to conform.

I was trying to decide between a dark green velvet dress and a pair of jeans and a T-shirt when Judy poked her head in my door.

"Granny, could I please borrow your blue overnight case? I need mine for the girls. Oh!" She stood in the doorway and stared at the piles of clothes cluttering every flat surface in the room.

I must have looked as discouraged as I felt, because she came right over and sat down on the bed beside me.

"What's the problem?"

"I have to take pictures at the school dance tonight and I don't know what to wear," I confessed.

"I see. Or maybe I don't. Why are you concerned about how you look if you're just going to be working?"

I didn't answer, but I guess my face gave me away.

"Oh, there's someone at the dance you want to impress, is there?" She smiled and stood up. "Well, how about we really make him sit up and

and take notice. Will you let me help?" I was desperate, so I nodded weakly. She smiled again. "Come on into my room and we'll start with the clothes."

An hour later I looked into her full-length mirror and had trouble identifying my own reflection. She had loaned me a soft turquoise sweater and miniskirt that looked great with my red hair. She even had the pantyhose and shoes to go with them. But the real renovation had come with her make-up job. Instead of pale gold, my eyes were framed with thick, dark lashes. Blue eyeliner and grey and blue shadow made them look twice as big as usual and sort of bluey-green. She had filled in my pale eyebrows with brown pencil and finished off the transformation with dark coral lipstick and blush. I had gone from black and white to living colour in one easy step.

I turned back to Judy to try and express my appreciation. "I don't know what to say, " I began.

"No need to say anything," she told me. "That's what I've been trying to get you to look like ever since I saw you come off that plane last summer. Now, about that suitcase . . ."

§   §   §

When I arrived at the school, the dance was barely started. The band was half-heartedly tuning up, and I was glad to see Gary in his usual spot at the back behind the drums. I vowed I'd get a word with him sometime during the evening and make my apologies for last Sunday. I should have left well enough alone.

I checked out my camera gear, made sure my flash was working okay, and began to circulate.

The first hour was pretty boring. Not many people showed up, and those who did were giggly ninth graders. Then, about nine-thirty half a dozen kids came in together and virtually took over the place. I stood back by the cloakroom doors and watched as Lonnie Kaye, clutching Steve possessively by the arm, marched with her entourage up to the front where a few tables were set up. The younger kids who had been sitting there got up and moved away, and Lonnie and her gang took over. More kids drifted in shortly after, and before ten minutes had passed the place was packed.

I had already taken nearly a whole roll of the ninth graders and the chaperones and the band — all very dull stuff. Now the action looked like it was starting in earnest, so I pulled out the first roll, reloaded, and went to work.

I purposely avoided Steve while I got some sensational shots of kids dancing, jumping for balloons, and all the stuff that seems to be normal for a high school party. Then, when I had two more rolls nearly finished, I went over to the centre table where he was sitting with Lonnie Kaye and a couple of other seniors and started shooting.

My first shot was of Lonnie Kaye surreptitiously hitching up her bra strap. When the flash went off, so did she.

"What the hell do you think you're doing?" she hissed.

"Just getting some candid shots for the paper," I replied sweetly, and turned the camera to the girl across from her who was gazing into space and blowing bubbles with a large wad of pink gum.

When he saw the first flash, Steve turned from the guy he was talking to and started to grin.

"Nice going, Granny. Anything you can get that's unusual will be great." He started to turn back, then did a perfect double-take. His head swivelled around and his mouth dropped open.

"Granny! I hardly recognized you. What did you do to yourself?" He stood up and came around the table to where I was standing to shoot another couple sharing a Coke and gazing into each other's eyes.

"Hi, Steve," I smiled and focussed again. "I hope you like the stuff I got. I've shot two rolls and I've just about finished the third."

"That should be lots," he mumbled. "Look, if you're through shooting, how about a dance?"

I depressed the shutter release button, turned off the flash, and gave him my best smile. "Love to, but let me put this stuff away first. I'll be right back." I walked quickly to the cloakroom and slipped my equipment into my camera bag. Then, I ran a comb through my hair and checked my unfamiliar eyes and lips. With one last glance, I went back into the gym.

Steve was waiting for me just inside the door. The band was playing "Send in the Clowns," and without a word he opened his arms and I walked into them. We started to dance and didn't stop until the band did half an hour later.

"Shouldn't you be getting back to your friends?" I asked as we slowly separated and stood looking at each other.

"Yeah, I guess so. But I don't really want to. Ah, maybe we could start again tomorrow night where we left off. Do you have any plans?"

"No, nothing I can't get out of," I replied, thinking how easy it would be to get out of watching an old movie on TV, which was what I had planned.

"Great. Then how about I pick you up around eight. We can take in a movie or whatever you want."

"I'd like that very much."

"You'd like *what* very much?" Lonnie's voice sliced through the mood that had been building.

Steve whirled around and half grinned at her. "Nothing, just discussing photography. You about ready to split?"

"I've been ready for the past half hour," she informed him tartly. "If you can tear yourself away from here, we can catch up to the others.

They're going to Tony's for pizza."

She glared at him for a second, then turned and walked to the door. Steve gave me a quick wink and a shrug and followed her.

I felt pretty let down after they left. Maureen and Toby had come in during the rush just after Lonnie and her gang made their entrance, but I hadn't had much chance to talk to them. Now I looked around and saw them standing over by the bandstand talking to Gary. I hurried across the floor. This would be a good chance to make that apology I'd promised myself.

"Hi," I called as I came up to them. "I've been wanting to talk to you."

Maureen and Toby turned around and stared at me. Gary looked down from his perch on the stage and snorted.

"Granny, you look incredible!" Maureen cried. "Boy, what a difference!"

"Yeah, Granny," Toby chimed in, "you're really something else. Isn't she, Gary?"

"Something else just about says it all," he replied, getting onto his feet and glaring down at me.

"What do you mean by that, Gary?" I whispered, feeling the anger he provoked so easily swelling up into my throat.

"Didn't anybody tell you this isn't a costume party? Who are you trying to be? Joan Collins?"

A bunch of kids near the stage giggled, and

I felt my anger turning to embarrassment.

"I don't think —"

"No, you don't, do you? I really thought I'd made a mistake about you, but once a phony, always a phony, I guess." He turned abruptly and walked over to his drums.

I stood for a moment in total disbelief, then as tears welled up in my eyes, I ran across the floor to the washroom.

"He didn't mean anything, Granny," Maureen soothed, slipping in the door behind me. "He's been in a foul mood all night and he was just taking it out on you. He'll apologize as soon as he sees you again."

"Oh, really? Well, I don't intend to give him the chance," I sniffed. I turned to the mirror and watched the tears leave a dark blue stream down my cheeks. "If I didn't have to work with him, I'd never see the wise guy again."

"Wise guy?" Maureen just barely managed to keep her laughter under control.

"It's not funny, Morrie. He embarrassed me in front of half the school. And now look at me. I could get a job with Ringling Brothers." Another cascade of blue, this time mixed with grey, gushed forth.

"Don't worry, I'll fix that in a sec. Where's your make-up?"

"At home," I muttered. "Judy put it on for me, and it never occurred to me that I'd need to do anything more to it."

"God, you are *so* naive! Well, sit down and I'll see what I can do with my stuff."

It was half an hour later before I was cleaned up and calmed down enough to go as far as the cloakroom for my coat and camera bag. Maureen got Toby while I waited outside. Ten minutes later they dropped me off at the house.

I was standing in the shower with my face up to the spray and vowing I'd never touch a mascara wand again in my entire life when I suddenly remembered my date with Steve. My anger at Gary disappeared instantly, replaced by a sudden rush of euphoria. Steve obviously thought my new look was just fine, and that was really all that mattered.

Chapter 17

I woke up early the next morning in a state of depression and panic. Excitement over my date with Steve was vying for mind control with gloom over how I would act and what I would wear and most of all how I would ever manage to look like I had last night without Judy's skilled touch. I had never properly appreciated her talents before.

After lying in a state of total paralysis for a few minutes, I finally decided I didn't need to worry about making up my face. Steve was used to seeing me *au naturel* and probably wouldn't expect the full drill for a movie date. Feeling a little better, I glanced at the clock — nine-fifteen, and I had three rolls of film to develop before noon. I jumped up and ran for the shower.

It was a little after eleven-thirty when I rushed into the editorial office with three sheets of prints. The first thing I saw as I came in the room was Steve and Gary at the layout table poring over copy. My heart gave an uncomfortable lurch, and I forced myself to walk over to them calmly.

"Here's the stuff from the dance last night," I murmured, holding the package of contact prints and negs out to Steve. "I hope they're what you want."

Steve glanced up, but he seemed to take a minute to focus on me. "Oh, er . . . yeah, fine, Granny. Give them to Gary, he'll be making the selection." Without further comment, he turned back to the spread.

"Here, I'll take them, Granny," Gary reached out his hand and gave me a half smile. But I was still looking at Steve, bewildered, and when I turned to face Gary, my mind replayed a quick video of the scene by the stage last night. I slapped the envelope down on the table in front of him.

"Fine!" I growled, and started for the door.

Maybe it was the anger in my voice that made Steve realize I was leaving. He looked up from the layouts and called, "Hey, wait a minute, Granny. We'll be finished here in an hour or so. Why don't you stick around and then drive down to the printer's with me? You really should see what happens to the stuff once it leaves here."

I turned back slowly. Steve was smiling encouragingly, and Gary was grimacing as if his feet hurt. My hurt and anger disappeared as quickly as they had come, and I smiled back at Steve in agreement. Gary grabbed my material and stormed into the darkroom.

An interesting contrast in personalities, I pondered as I sank into a chair behind Toby Tubbs' desk. A moment later Toby himself roared in and handed Steve his copy of the article that would accompany my pictures for the centre spread. I moved to the chair across the desk, and we started talking, and I soon forgot all about what had happened.

Half an hour later Gary came out of the darkroom with a handful of two by three prints. Without a glance my way, he plunked them down on Steve's desk.

"I picked out ten usable shots. You and Daniels can arrange them any way you like. I've outlined where they should go on the page so you shouldn't have any trouble." He nodded curtly to Steve, ignored me, and left the room.

Curious as to what Gary thought was "usable," I sauntered over to Steve's desk and looked down as he laid them out on the page. I couldn't believe what I was seeing. Gary had picked out ten of the tamest shots I had taken. No Lonnie fixing her strap, no bubble gum popper, no lovers gazing at each other — nothing of any real appeal. Just ordinary shots of kids grabbing for balloons and chaperones looking slightly bored.

I turned to Steve in horror.

"He deliberately didn't blow up my best shots, Steve. I had some great stuff of —"

Steve shook his head. "Yeah, I remember. I

guess Gary thought they were too intimate or something. He *was* right about those pictures of the faculty though," he grinned. "At any rate, there's nothing we can do about it now. This stuff has to be down to Joe Daniels' shop by two. No time to make any changes at this late date." He gathered up the huge folder with the copy, tucked it under his arm, and smiled. "Ready?"

What else could I do? I followed him meekly out the door.

Joe Daniels gave me a tour of the print shop after he and Steve had gone over the copy in his office. The whole operation was fascinating and I was filled with questions.

"Let's go for a burger and discuss it," Steve suggested after Joe had finished with me. "I haven't had lunch, and I'll bet you haven't either."

At the mention of food, my stomach sent up a loud moan. Steve grinned and took my arm. "I thought so. Come on, there's a great little place just around the corner." He took my arm and led me out the door.

As soon as we were seated on stools behind an atrocious purple counter, Steve looked over at me and frowned.

"I didn't realize how pale you are, Granny. Are you feeling okay?"

"Yes, I'm fine," I answered, puzzled.

"Well, you sure look washed out. Maybe it's just that you're not wearing any make-up."

"I hardly ever wear make-up, just on special occasions. You've never mentioned it before," I pointed out, feeling very uncomfortable.

"I guess that's because I didn't realize what a difference it makes. You should wear it all the time."

So much for *au naturel*. Suddenly food lost its appeal, and all I could think of was getting home and practising. If only I could remember which came first, the eye liner or the mascara. And what brush had Judy used for the shadow?

§ § §

When I arrived home at four, Judy and the twins had already left for the airport and Dad was sitting in his den reading the latest *Photography* magazine. I ran directly upstairs and into Judy's room. She had taken most of her make-up, but there was still more than I would ever need. I sat down at her dressing table and started experimenting. At five-thirty I gave up and admitted that there was more to creating a new face that I'd managed to absorb in my twenty-minute workout with Judy last night. I needed help — Morrie.

I persuaded her to come over and help without too much trouble. But before she had finished, I began to wonder if it had been a good idea. Remember, Maureen is into heavy drama. By the time Steve came for me at eight, she had made me into someone else entirely by introducing me to the exotic world of silver eye shadow and vivid lipstick. I wasn't sure if I liked what I saw.

But Steve seemed to like the results, if I could judge by the admiring whistle he gave when I opened the door for him. As a matter of fact, he was a little too enthusiastic for Dad, who came out into the hall just as Steve was putting an arm possessively around my shoulder.

"Ahem," was his opening comment.

I pulled away from Steve and turned a very embarrassed face to Dad.

"Ah, this is Steve Williams, the editor of the *Speaker*. My father, Gordon Tyler."

"Pleased to meet you, sir." Steve put out his hand and smiled.

Dad took his hand and didn't smile back. He was looking at me strangely. I guess he wasn't too impressed with the new me.

"Where are you two going?" he finally asked, sounding like he thought Steve might be taking me to a drug hang-out.

"Just to a movie," Steve answered, "and maybe a pizza after."

"Very well. Granada, I want you home by eleven o'clock. Have a nice time." He was back in his den before I could protest the early curfew.

The movie Steve chose was at a drive-in down near the border. It took nearly an hour to get there, and what with buying tickets, trying to find an empty spot, and fortifying ourselves with sodas and chips, the movie was half over by the time we were settled. Not that it mattered. It seems that North Americans don't go to drive-ins to see movies anyway.

I had just nicely settled down and reached out to adjust the speaker when I was pulled not too gently over to the middle of the seat. Steve had his arms around me and his mouth on the back of my neck before I could even get my hand back through the window. And then he was kissing and fondling and stroking me all in different places. This was not like our earlier Coke dates!

I found myself enjoying it, but confused. My total experience in making out with a boy had been one wet kiss that just missed my mouth from the younger brother of my roommate in Switzerland. I know that must sound incredible, but unfortunately I had never dated anyone who wasn't extrememly gentlemanly and proper toward me, probably because I was a friend of their sister or the daughter of someone their parents knew. At any rate, I felt just like I'd suddenly landed in the middle of an X-rated movie.

My biggest problem was that I wasn't sure what to do in return. But Steve didn't seem to notice my inactivity. He just carried on with his kissing and other forms of entertainment. Whenever the action got too intense, I pulled away and stuffed a few chips in my mouth, which served to cool him down quite nicely. But he always started up again before long. All in all it was a very satisfying experience, and one I would have been quite happy to carry on. But during one lull I glanced at my watch and realized that it was after ten-thirty already.

"Steve," I cried, "we've got to leave right now! We'll never make it home on time."

"But the movie isn't over," he complained.

I thought he was being funny. "You're right, how foolish of me," I answered. "It doesn't matter, we've got to get moving. Maybe you can catch the ending on the late show."

He didn't laugh. "Come on, Granny, don't be a drag. We're just starting to get to know one another."

I was starting to get panicky. On the one hand, I didn't want to turn Steve off now that he was finally getting seriously interested in me. But on the other hand, I didn't want Dad angry with me. I knew he trusted me, and I was determined I wouldn't do anything to make him lose that trust.

"We can get to know each other on the drive home," I insisted. "If you don't get me home at a decent time, Dad will never let me go out with you again." It was a risk, but luckily it worked.

"Okay, you win." He moved over behind the wheel and started the engine. "Better take a Kleenex to your face," he suggested.

I tipped the rearview mirror and stared in horror. The Morrie original that had been created from my face now looked like a little kid's finger painting. I scrubbed away the mess as well as I could while Steve manoeuvered the car out of the drive-in and back onto the highway. It was certainly easier to be pale and uninteresting.

The drive home wasn't calculated to further our knowledge of one another after all. Steve hardly said a word, and I was too worried about Dad to encourage conversation. When we finally pulled up in front of our house at twenty-five to twelve, I was out the door and up the walk almost before the tires had stopped turning. Steve caught me at the front door and tried to begin a rerun of the scene at the drive-in.

"Steve, please, I've got to get in before my fa—" Too late. The door opened and Dad stood in the hall glaring at us.

"I thought I told you to have my daughter home by eleven. It's nearly twenty to twelve."

"I'm very sorry, sir," Steve apologized, dropping his hands from my shoulders. "The movie ran late and it took a little longer to drive home that I had anticipated. Believe me, it won't happen again."

Dad didn't bother to answer. "Come in, Granada," he ordered.

I gave Steve a fleeting smile and followed my father's rigid back into the house.

"I don't want you to think I'm coming on like a heavy parent, Granny," Dad said, putting his arm around me and walking me to the kitchen. "But, honey, you haven't had much experience with boys like Steve. Look what you've done to yourself for him tonight; that's not you. I feel I have to protect you, I guess. I'm sorry if I embarrassed you out there."

I was so relieved that he wasn't angry with me for being late that I didn't really pay much attention to his other comments. It wasn't until I was in bed half an hour and three pieces of cinnamon toast later that I thought about them.

What had Dad meant by "boys like Steve"? Was Steve diferent from other boys? Of course he was; that's why I had been working so hard to make him like me. And it looked like I was finally succeeding. Tonight's look might not have been what Dad was used to, but Steve had sure liked it!

Was there anything wrong with wanting Steve to like me? No, Dad was wrong to worry. I knew what I was doing. I wasn't so naive that I didn't know enough to keep out of trouble. I could handle myself without Dad's protection. And with any luck, I would.

Chapter 18

But I didn't get a chance to have to protect myself for a while. I didn't even see Steve in the next few days. I tried not to let it worry me, but of course it did. Had Dad's attitude driven him away? I could only hope not, and try to let him know that I was still interested inspite of Dad's abruptness on Saturday.

That's why I slipped down to the *Speaker* office during my free third period on Tuesday. I hoped to find Steve there and have a chance to talk to him, but no one was in the office. I did find something else though. A big bundle of the new edition of the *Speaker* was sitting just inside the door, ready to be distributed during the lunch hour. I picked up a copy and opened it to the centre page.

The first thing that jumped out at me was my name in big letters under the photo spread, and I felt a little wave of euphoria. Then I looked at the pictures and the euphoria was quickly replaced with disappointment and anger — disappointment that my first big piece was so mundane and anger at Gary for shafting me. I folded the paper shut without bothering to read any of Toby's write-up and started to put it back in the bundle when a boxed item on the front page caught my eye.

Attention
all you amateur photographers!

The third annual high school photography contest is again being sponsored by the Vancouver Herald. As you probably remember from last year, each Vancouver and district high school is allowed only one entry. All entrants will then compete for the top prize of a trip to Montreal for the national finals. In addition, the local winner will receive a gift certificate for $300 from Hall's Photo Palace.

So get that Baby Brownie out of mothballs, all you shutterbugs, and give it your best shot. The theme this year is "The Class of 2000" — in other words, the playschool set. Entries should consist of at least six photos and must be in to the Speaker *office by November 25.*

I read the paragraph over twice to be sure I had it straight in my mind. A photo contest and only one entry per school. Here it was — a perfect chance to get back at Gary O'Hare!

I spent the rest of the study period planning the photos I would take. I would go over to the elementary school during lunch hour and get some shots of the kindergarten kids. And there was a park just down the block where the little guys hung out on the swings and teeter-totters and carousel. That should be good for a bunch of interesting candids.

Then it suddenly came to me. I already had a portfolio of candid shots of little children — the pictures I took of Trina and Trixie. They were obviously good enough to interest the people at Tiny Tammy, and Dad himself thought some of them were exceptional. I'd get the negs, pick out the best, and get Dad to help me work magic with special filters and paper.

As soon as the bell rang I rushed to the cafeteria to find Morrie and tell her about the contest and how I was finally going to get even with Gary O'Hare. Strangely, she wasn't nearly as thrilled about the prospect as I was.

"I really don't understand you, Granny. I thought you and Gary were getting along so well when we went to the concert. Now here you are furious with him again just because he made a slightly critical remark about your looks."

"Slightly critical! He made me look stupid in front of half the high school. But that's not why I'm so mad at him. It's what he did with my photo spread." I pulled the rumpled copy of the *Speaker* out of my notebook and opened it for her to see.

"So what's wrong with that? I think they're really good."

"Oh, Morrie, they're the dullest shots I took. I had some great stuff of Lonnie Kaye and her crowd, but he didn't use one of them."

"Oh?" She gave me a funny look. "And what were they?"

"Just some unusual candid pictures," I hedged. For some reason I didn't want to describe them to her.

What was the matter with me? I had been so proud of those pictures; at least, I thought I had. But when it came to talking about them, I suddenly realized how embarrassing they were. Did I want them printed because I thought they were such hotshot material, or did I just want Lonnie Kaye Borgnine to be laughed at? I had a horrible feeling I already knew the answer to that one.

Gary, as usual, had been right, I realized, which made me even more determined to beat him in the photo contest. Sure it was illogical, but did I ever say I thought in straight lines?

"Anyway," I said, picking up a tray and getting into the food line-up, "I'm entering that contest and I'm going to win. That's a promise."

"Well, good luck. But you'll have pretty stiff competition. Gary won the local competition last year and was runner-up in the national. I think he's pretty determined to take first place again."

"We'll see." I smiled to myself and took something that looked vaguely like a science experiment from the dessert section.

For the rest of the week Dad and I worked on the negatives, trying out all sorts of techniques like dodging to hold back part of the face tones. We also fooled around with posterization and using texture screens and double printing to obtain unusual results. I certainly learned a lot about the creativity of the darkroom during that time. I also learned how much learning I still had to do to be even a good amateur.

Whenever I wasn't in the darkrooom with Dad, I was thinking hard about Steve. I had at least managed to see him by now, but he had been pretty cool with me, as if our hot date last Saturday had never happened. I couldn't figure it out. One day he could hardly keep his hands off me, but the next week he practically ignored me. Why the sudden change?

The answer came to me after Judy and the twins came home from Halifax late Thursday. Seeing Judy and hearing her talk about how much work she had done to prepare the twins for their interviews made me realize that on Friday and Saturday night I had put a lot of work into my appearance too. But since then I had gone back to being just plain Granny. Maybe now that Steve had seen a different me he didn't appreciate the old one any more.

So I determined to make that different me the one he saw every day. I bought loads of make-up and spent hours working with it until

I had developed a new look I was sure Steve would like — lots of colour and a little glitz. Then I went a step further and got myself a punk hairdo and a few way-out clothes. That should work to catch Steve's interest.

Things were a little different for me during the week after that. I introduced the new me at school on Monday and realized how right it was. Boys who had never noticed me before started asking to sit with me in the caf and to drive me home after school. And there were a lot of other invitations too. But the only invitation I wanted to hear was one from Steve.

And it came. As I had hoped, his interest in me had picked up again with my new look, and on Friday we went out on our second real date. At last I had another chance to redeem myself.

I won't bore you with the details, because the date was a repeat performance of the last one — same script, different location. This time we passed on the movie and drove directly to Stanley Park. We parked the car near Second Beach and resumed where we had left off at the drive-in. It was a little more difficult to control Steve though, since I didn't have any munchies to break the spell with. But when he got a little too insistent, I threatened to get out and walk home. I had kept Dad's words in mind and carefully worked out that plan in case I needed it. It worked too. After a little argument, Steve apologized and sat back and really talked to me for another half hour. Then he drove me home.

I was a little disappointed that he didn't take the opportunity to ask me to go with him to the big football game that was coming up, but I was hoping he would ask me soon. Getting Dad to agree to it was what I would have to worry about.

You see, the football game is really a football weekend, because it happens out of town. It's a traditional grudge match between Fi High and St. Laurence in Victoria. It meant taking the ferry over on Saturday morning in time for the game at two o'clock, then dinner at the Empress Hotel and a big dance afterwards. We wouldn't come back until the next afternoon. But everyone at school told me that the whole thing was always well chaperoned, so I was counting on being able to persuade Dad. I figured it would be a wonderful weekend, especially if I went with Steve.

So things were going well for me. The only fly in my ointment, as they say, was Gary. When I realized that Tuesday that he was probably right about the candid shots of Lonnie Kaye, I was angry. But after a week spent plotting his downfall in the photo contest, my anger had cooled. So on Monday I decided to try to make up with him.

I saw him in the cafeteria at lunch time and went over to talk to him. But before I reached him he looked at me with disgust in his eyes, then turned to the two boys he was with and started making crude remarks about Boy George look-alikes. And he stayed downright rude like that all week. His attitude made it easy for me to want to beat the pants off him in the contest. I went back to my work in the darkroom with renewed vigour.

Oh, there was one other fly — Judy. She had to wait at least a week before she would hear the results of the Tiny Tammy contest, and it was purgatory around the house in the meantime. She came back from Halifax not nearly as sure that the twins were a shoo-in as she was when she left. Apparently the P.R. guys who were handling the contest were not exactly knocked out by the girls, and she couldn't understand why the change in attitude. The president had been so high on the twins, and then the people who would make the final choice came on pretty cool.

It was obvious to me that the judges were not thrilled with the way Judy had the girls all made up for their interviews. I couldn't help but wish we'd told her about my pictures at the very beginning. It would have hurt her to think that all her ideas about the girls were for the birds, but at least she might have been willing to let them be natural for their interview. Now it looked like she really blew it and I couldn't help bur feel that it was at least partly my fault.

The idea bothered me, but most of the time

my head was too full of the good things going on in my life to worry about it much.

§ § §

I had been a little disappointed about Steve not mentioning another date when he brought me home on Friday, but my disappointment didn't last long. On Sunday, he called about noon and asked me to go for a ride with him. We drove out of town and stopped at a bluff overlooking the ocean.

"So are you going to Victoria with me?" Steve's voice broke into my admiration of the view.

The seagulls were screaming at the waves, and I wasn't sure I had heard him properly.

"What did you say?"

"Look, Granny, I guess you've been wondering where you stand. Well, I had a few ends to tie up before I could start dating you formally, but I broke up with Lonnie Kaye last night. As of now I'm free. I'd like to get to know you a lot better, and I'd like you to come with me to the football game in Victoria."

I was overwhelmed. It was what I'd been hoping for since last September when I saw him standing behind the *Speaker* recruiting booth. I couldn't believe it had all worked out just as I'd planned.

Before I could make any sort of reply, Steve had his arms around me and his mouth was doing its interesting stuff. When we finally came up for air a half hour later, he said, "You haven't answered me yet. Will you go to the football bash with me?"

"I guess so," I answered happily. "But I'll have to check with my father first."

"If you think he'll give you any flack about going with me, just tell him you'll be well chaperoned. And your friend, Maureen Whats-her-name, will be going, won't she? I heard Toby talking to her about it the other day."

"Yes, she's going," I murmured. But now that it came right down to it, I was wondering how much luck I would have persuading Dad to let me go. He still wasn't as crazy about Steve as I was. In fact, he was still promoting Gary whenever he got the chance.

Steve smiled. "Wonderful. I'm really looking forward to us being able to get to know each other much better on this trip." And he drew me close and began again on my neck.

I decided I didn't want to probe into that one any deeper, especially not right now. So I suggested we drive down to Granville Island and get something to eat. It wasn't that I was starving — not after three stacks of french toast and a breakfast steak. But I was getting a little uncomfortable with all the heavy breathing.

When we got home a couple of hours later, I suggested that Steve come in and meet Judy and the twins. It was not one of my better moves. The five of us had just got settled over glasses of juice in the kitchen when the back door opened and Dad and Gary O'Hare came in.

"Oh, you're home," Dad observed rather unnecessarily.

The air suddenly felt like there was an electric storm going on right in the kitchen. Gary stood in the middle of the floor and glared first at Steve, then at me, then back at Steve. I started to offer him a glass of juice, but he ignored me and turned to my father. "Thanks for the suggestions, Mr. Tyler," he muttered, then walked back out the door.

Dad did not look pleased. Without acknowledging Steve's presence, he went out into the hall and up the stairs. Judy looked as baffled as I felt, and the twins looked frightened. Only Steve took the whole thing calmly.

"Guess Gary's not too happy to see me," he grinned. "Poor guy, he's really got it bad for you."

"Me? You must be nuts! Gary hates the ground that I walk on!"

"Yeah? That's not the way I see it." He took a last swallow of his juice and stood up. "Nice to meet you, Mrs. Tyler. I'd better be going now. I've got a history paper due tomorrow that I've got to get started on." He turned and gave me a quick kiss on the mouth. "Let me know soon about the weekend, eh?"

The twins giggled, Judy's mouth dropped open, and I turned red. Then he was gone.

Chapter 19

That was Sunday.

Monday and Tuesday I spent walking on air and grinning like a toothpaste ad. Steve started driving me to school and sitting with me at lunch. He even walked me to a couple of my classes with his arm around my waist. Girls I hardly knew gave me envious glances. It was right out of *Sweet Valley High*.

Then came Wednesday. On a scale of one to a hundred, Wednesday would have been too low for the scale. All it needed was a little nuclear fallout to make it a complete disaster.

That morning Steve drove me to school as usual, but on our way to my first class we ran into Lonnie Kaye. The look she gave me was bad enough, but what she laid on Steve should have zapped him into the next building. He pretended not to notice anything was wrong and, smiling at her, said, "Hey, how's it going, Lonnie?"

Her face kind of crumpled and she rushed into the nearest room. Unfortunately, so did a group of ninth graders. Steve started to frown and shake his head.

"Gee, I didn't think she'd be so upset," I remarked.

"She really shouldn't take it so hard," Steve answered. "After all, we weren't engaged or anything."

The whole scene put kind of a damper on the pleasure I was getting out of my new status. I spoke to Maureen about it during lunch, thinking she would be able to get me thinking straight again. It didn't work out quite the way I'd hoped.

"Look, Granny, I know you had your heart set on going steady with Steve Williams and I'm glad for you that you made it. But remember, Lonnie and Steve have been an item for almost three years now. It can't be that easy, especially for someone like Lonnie, to get dumped. She's been the Queen of the Starlight Ballroom since grade school; she just isn't used to losing out."

I couldn't believe what I was hearing. "You mean I should be feeling sorry for that spoiled little snob who has never spoken a civil word to me since I came to this school? You've got to be kidding!"

"Yeah, I know, she's been giving you a hard time. But maybe that was her only defense. Oh, never mind, let's skip it. It's too hard to explain."

After that great note of encouragement from my best friend, I started the afternoon in a black cloud. Then came last period gym.

The class was divided into six groups to work out on the various pieces of equipment —

the horse, the trapeze and so forth. I was in the group at the parallel bars executing a handstand when I felt the inside of my nose give a kind of gush and blood begin to pour. I flipped myself back on my feet and ran for the washroom.

I was concentrating so hard on getting the bleeding stopped that I didn't realize at first that someone else was there. It wasn't till I turned off the cold water that I heard the quiet sobbing in one of the booths behind me. I turned around just as the door opened and Lonnie Kaye Borgnine came out into the room.

Her eyes were red and she was clutching a wadded tissue. But when she saw me she threw her head in the air and straightened her back.

"You!" she whispered. "I suppose you saw me come in here and couldn't wait to see what was wrong. Well, lucky you, you caught me. I hope you're satisfied."

"No, I wasn't looking for you," I stammered. "I had this nose bleed and . . ." To my utter horror all her bravado was disappearing as I spoke. Her faced crumpled and she started to sob.

"Why did you have to come to this school anyway? There are thousands of high schools in Canada, why did you have to pick this one!"

"I didn't —"

"I knew that first day I saw you trying to sign up for the paper that you were out to take Steve away from me. I didn't think you had a chance at first, but then you started to dazzle him with your camera work for the paper. And as if that wasn't enough, you suddenly turned into Madonna."

She pulled out a paper towel and ran water on it. Then she faced me again. "But you're a phony, Granny, and it won't be long before Steve realizes it. And then you'll be the one crying in the washroom." She turned back to the mirror and started to repair the tear damage.

"Look, Lonnie, I'm sorry if Steve prefers me, but that's the way it is." I was starting to get mad. "And I'm not phony!"

She gave a sad laugh. "No? What do you call it then? All that heavy make-up and the short skirts and spiked hair? Don't you realize how unreal you are?"

I wanted to leave before she could say anything more, but my feet didn't seem to understand the message my brain was sending out.

"Just don't think for one minute that Steve is going to be taken in by you forever, Granada. He'll get tired of you just like he's gotten tired of every other cheap girl he's thought about in the past three years. Then good luck finding anyone else to date you who isn't into black leather and iron chains." She dropped the wet towel in the garbage, then tossed her head and marched out of the room.

I stood rooted to the spot for a good five minutes. Then slowly I walked out to my locker, changed into my blouse and skirt, and left the building.

Since Steve had driven me to school, I didn't have my bike. It was just as well. I needed time to think, and the half hour walk home gave it to me. Could Lonnie really be right? Was I turning into a phony? And did my looks make that much difference in how Steve felt about me?

No, I tried to tell myself, he had shown an interest in me long before I started to fix myself up. But if I was honest I had to admit it hadn't been very serious until I'd deliberately decided to change my looks to suit him. He had always been more interested in my photography and the paper than anything else until lately. Maybe there was something to what Lonnie said.

But Lonnie was jealous and using every weapon in her arsenal to fight me. I couldn't let her make me lose my confidence. Steve chose me over her, and that made me the winner.

Or did it? Lonnie's tragic face kept projecting itself on my brain. She really was broken up about losing Steve; Morrie said they had been an item for a long time. If only I understood the dynamics of teenage dating a little better.

I was still feeling pretty punk about the whole thing when I walked into the house and down to the kitchen. I could hear Judy talking on the phone.

"I just don't understand it, Gordon. The letter is so curt. Just 'Sorry but we've chosen someone else.' No explanation, nothing."

I slipped out of my sweater and dropped into a chair by the table to wait.

"Isn't there anything I can do?" Pause. "No, I suppose not. But the president was so high on the girls. I just don't understand it." Another pause. "Well, I'll try. See you tonight." She hung up the phone and turned around. "Hello, Granny," she murmured quietly. Then she sank down in a chair across from me.

"Bad news?" I asked, knowing perfectly well what the news was.

"The girls didn't win the Tiny Tammy contest. This came in the afternoon mail." She threw the letter down on the table and sighed. "I simply don't understand it."

I watched the emotions play over her face — confusion, disappointment, sadness. And I suddenly realized that I had to tell her the truth, no matter what.

"Judy, you'll probably be furious with me when you hear this, but you have to know. The pictures of the girls that got them into the finals weren't the studio portraits you had done. They were the candid shots I took when you and Dad were in Washington that weekend."

She shook her head. "You mean those funny pictures of the girls in their bathing suits and nightgowns?" A little smile crept across her lips. "They were cute, weren't they? But, Granny, I took those pictures down to be framed. The studio pictures went to the Tiny Tammy people."

"No, Judy, my candids went too. Dad found the negs and blew them up, then picked out the best and sent them to the president of the company himself. That's why he was so keen on the girls." I went on to explain the mix-up with the telegram and the phone call.

"So it really was those candid shots that got them to Halifax," I concluded. "We tried to warn you to lay off the artificial stuff and let the girls be natural, but you didn't want to hear it. I guess we should have been more blunt, then maybe the girls would have won the contest. I'm sorry."

"But why are you telling me this now? The girls already lost their big chance. I blew it for them. What good will it do now?"

"Just this. The twins are adorable just the way they are. They're naturals. And there are lots of other contests. Just let them be themselves and they're sure to be winners."

"You really think so?"

"I *know* so." I smiled.

She sat for a moment longer, looking uncertain, then she jumped up from the table and began scrambling through a pile of papers on the kitchen counter.

"Here, look at this," she said, handing me a clipping from a newspaper.

I read it over quickly. It was a notice about a contest a local department store was sponsoring to find Miss Vancouver of 2000.

"Do you think maybe I should submit a few of those pictures you took, Granny?"

"I sure do, Judy. And I'll bet my wide-angle lens they'll win this time."

She came over and put her arms around me. "Thanks, Granny. I guess I've known all along that you and Gordon were right about the twins. But I wanted so badly to have them win that I just wouldn't recognize it. I guess I forgot how important it is to be yourself."

I hugged her back and escaped to my room before the dam broke. It was the first time Judy had ever hugged me. She'd always been warm and friendly but never openly affectionate. I guess we were both afraid to let ourselves go with each other. It felt wonderful.

I would have been riding on cloud nine as I stood there if I hadn't begun to realize that she'd hit the nail on the head for me too. "How important it is to be yourself." I had done to myself exactly what I'd been trying to stop her from doing to Trixie and Trina.

I went into the bathroom, looked at myself in the mirror, and saw for the first time what everyone else must have seen all along. Lonnie was probably right — Steve was bowled over by the crazy look I'd taken on, but it would never last. Everything about me was as big a lie as my first photos had been.

Dad had tried to suggest that I was going a little overboard, and Gary had certainly been blunt enough about what he thought of the new me. But it wasn't just my looks. Lots of kids dressed and made up like that. The problem was that on me it was all wrong. I was trying to be someone I wasn't, simply to attract a boy I didn't really know anything about.

I thought of the few dates Steve and I had had and realized that we did nothing but make out. And the football weekend was shaping up to be just another version of the same, only this time it would probably be X-rated.

Then there was the way he had dumped Lonnie. She was right — the same thing would be happening to me before long. And I didn't like that idea one little bit.

I thought for a moment longer, then picked up the phone and dialed the number I had memorized last September.

Chapter 20

I stayed home from school the next day on the pretext of feeling a cold coming on. I just couldn't face anyone yet; I needed time to get my thinking straightened out.

But that wasn't my only pretext. When I phoned Steve Wednesday evening it was to tell him that my father wouldn't let me go on the football weekend. This, I promised myself, would be my last conscious lie. I hadn't even asked Dad for permission, but I needed an excuse to get out of what I knew would be a situation I just wasn't ready to handle.

When I biked to school Friday morning, after assuring Steve that I was okay and didn't want a ride, I was pretty apprehensive as to the reception I would get. Gone was the heavy eye make-up, gone was the spiky hair, gone were the short leather skirt and tight T-shirt. I hadn't quite gone back to the old Granada, though. I'd darkened my brows and lashes and put on a fairly bright lipstick. Judy was right about me needing a bit of colour. But I certainly looked a lot different than I had two days before.

Maureen was the first person I saw as I came up the stairs to the front door just as the last bell sounded. Although I hadn't told her what had happened, she knew I was having problems. When I hadn't shown up at school the previous day, she'd phoned to see if I was okay. I told her I was fine and would be in school the next day, and I guess she gathered I'd need moral support. She was waiting for me.

"Holy moly, Granny, what happened to you? I thought you said you weren't sick."

"I just got rid of a little excess baggage," I replied, feeling very uncomfortable. "Do I look okay?"

She scrutinized me very carefully as we went down the hall to homeroom. Then, just as we were going through the door, she announced her decision. "Actually, you don't look as bad as I thought at first. Not as interesting as before, but on the other hand it's more you."

That was just what I wanted to hear.

I had expected a lot of comments from the kids in my classes, but no one else said anything all morning.

I guess it's true that people are far more concerned about *their* image than yours.

It was during lunch that I got my second reaction, this time from Lonnie Kaye. I expected her to make some derogatory comment in a Lear jet voice which would embarrass me in front of half the student body. But no. I was carrying my tray over to a vacant window table where I would be relatively isolated when she came through the door and saw me. I waited for the shriek and hoped it wouldn't break my juice glass. Instead she merely stopped in her tracks and looked me up and down. Then, while I waited for a caustic comment, she murmured, "Your outfit looks great, Granada. I wish I could wear green." As she marched off, I swear she grew at least a few centimetres. Obviously I'd made her day. I guess she figured I'd stopped being a threat so she could start being human.

I knew I was going to have to face Steve sooner or later, and I dreaded running into him between classes. So I spent the entire day skulking along the halls like a fugitive. But when the final bell rang, I made my way reluctantly down to the *Speaker* office for the bi-weekly staff conference.

As soon as I saw Steve I started to regret my decision to turn down the Victoria trip. He was wearing a pale blue wool sweater that made his eyes look almost navy, and a lock of his hair was hanging over his forehead like a little kid. I saw with regret that the rest of the staff was already there. I wouldn't have a chance to speak with him.

Everyone looked up when I walked in. Steve frowned, and I didn't know if it was because of the way I looked or because I was late. "Sit down, Granny," he ordered, and I took the only vacant chair which, wouldn't you know, was next to Gary O'Hare.

"We're running through the special features for the next edition. Naturally, the major part of the paper will be taken up with a report on the Victoria weekend." He shuffled the papers in front of him and looked away from me. "Since you won't be going to the bash, Toby will help Gary with the camera work."

Suddenly all my new-found pride in myself deserted me, and it was all I could do not to stand up and shout, "Of course I'm going to Victoria. It was just a joke." But one look at Steve's tight lips stopped that clever impulse.

"You'll be the only staff person who isn't in Victoria, so I'd like you to cover the home ec bake-off in family studies. A couple of our students are competing with students from three other schools in the district for the title of Point Grey Cookie Queen."

Great!

I could feel myself deflating into my chair, and I turned my head sideways so I wouldn't have to see Steve's stern face. As I did, I caught Gary devouring me with his eyes. I expected to see scorn and self-righteousness, but instead I saw genuine sympathy and something that looked a whole lot like affection. As soon as he caught my eye, though, the scowl returned, and I decided I must have been imagining the whole thing.

I spent the rest of the meeting silently cursing myself for being such a sap and trying to think of a way to get back my chance to go to Victoria. Nothing very original came to mind, so I was forced, when the meeting was over, to go up to Steve and try out another lie.

"Dad's changed his mind about the Victoria trip, Steve. He says I can go."

He stood up and started sorting through his papers without looking at me. "That's great, Granny," he muttered. "The only thing is, since you copped out I made other plans. I asked Barbe Neil to go with me."

Well, at least he wasn't taking Lonnie Kaye. That would have been just too much of a blow to my pride. Barbe Neil is not serious competition. She's sixteen going on thirty, in grade nine. She looks like a high-priced call girl and has the IQ of a bright tadpole. I decided to play it cool, as Maureen says.

"That's okay. I really just wanted to go to help with the photography. So if it's okay with you, I'll take Toby's place and maybe one of the younger kids can cover the home ec thing."

I smiled and waited for his agreement.

He finally looked up and faced me. I knew before he spoke what he was going to say. "Sorry, Granny, the assignments have all been given out. Unless you can talk Gary into it, you'll stay covering the home ec contest."

His voice was cold, but his eyes gave him

away. They were sad and confused. I guess I'd hurt him more than I ever dreamed I could. After all, here was I, a lowly sophomore, turning down an invitation from the king of Fi High. His pride, probably for the first time in his life, must have been positively destroyed.

But what about mine? I'd tried to fix things up and gotten squashed for my effort. As I watched him move swiftly away, I realized just how much I still had to learn about men. Boy, how I wished Mlle. Garnon's Academy for Young Ladies had been co-ed!

I don't think I would have felt like such a first class jerk if Gary hadn't witnessed the whole thing. When I finally stirred myself and stood up, I could see him out of the corner of my eye standing by the door to the darkroom.

"Just don't say anything," I warned, feeling the anger at Steve wash away any embarrassment I felt.

"Okay," he grinned, "but I was just going to offer you the Victoria assignment. Steve said it was up to me, and you're by far the best photographer we've got."

This was sure my day for stunned disbelief.

"You mean that?" I asked, half waiting for the put-down I was sure would follow.

"Absolutely. You can travel with Toby and me if you don't mind my old Volvo — Maureen will be with us too. The school booked rooms for us; Maureen's is a single, but Toby and I can switch and give you girls our double."

"Why are you doing this, Gary?" I asked suspiciously.

He shrugged. "As I said, you're the best photographer on the paper, maybe in the whole city."

Now I really did feel embarrassed. "Well, thanks very much. Of course I'll take you up on the offer. I'm sure Dad will let me go if he knows I'll be with you and Maureen."

He looked puzzled. "I thought you just told Steve your dad had changed his mind and okayed the trip."

See what a mess lying can get you in? I decided that since I couldn't remember to cover my tracks, I'd better just go for the truth.

"As a matter of fact, I haven't actually spoken to Dad about it. I told Steve I couldn't go because . . . well, never mind why. Then when it looked like I was going to miss out on such a terrific assignment, I made up that story about him changing his mind."

"At it again, eh?" He shook his head and frowned.

"What? Oh, you mean my tendency to somewhat embellish the facts. Yeah, I know, it's not smart. But I've made a solemn vow never to say or do a deceitful thing again." He just stared down at me. "If you can believe it," I grinned up at him.

Gradually his scowl turned to a smile. "Well,

for what it's worth, I see you've made a good start." His eyes did a tour from my head to my sneakers. "You look nice, Granada," he murmured, then turned almost as red as his hair.

Chapter 21

The football weekend went exactly as planned. I went with Morrie, Toby and Gary, and did all the things a good photographer covering a major story does. At the game Gary worked the players and I took candid shots of the fans. We got a lot of fine shots for the paper.

Then came the evening of the banquet and dance. It was understood that the four of us would go together, and although I knew Gary would probably make a lot of snide comments, I dressed to the teeth and put on a heavier dose of make-up than I had been wearing.

I was shooting for Linda Evans rather than Joan Collins, and I guess I must have come pretty close. Even Gary didn't make any derogatory comments. In fact, when I came down to the lobby with Maureen to meet the boys, he actually whistled. I was very flattered, but he was *not* my target.

At the banquet we were seated at tables for eight, so it wasn't until two hours later at the dance that I came face to face with Steve. He looked fantastic in his dinner jacket, and I could feel my heart beginning to pound even before he spoke.

"Well, well, Granny, so you decided to come after all. I can't tell you how great this is." He was gazing down at me, half surprised, half admiring. Barbe was clinging to his arm as though she were afraid he might drift off into the air if she let go, and glaring at me in perfect imitation of Lonnie Kaye. And just to complete the scene, the orchestra started playing "Send in the Clowns."

Instant replay of the Fall Fling.

I smiled up at Steve, and he gently untangled his arm from Barbe's clutches and said, "I think they're playing our song."

Honestly!

Gary was standing behind me, obviously taking the whole thing in and sending out enough steam to unwrinkle the back of my dress.

"Why, so they are," I answered. My heart was making so much noise I was sure the whole ballroom could hear it. "I just love dancing to it." I smiled up at him again, but as he reached out to take my arm, I turned around to Gary and said, "Do you want to lead or shall I?"

Gary's face broke into a grin and he took my hand. "I will," he said. "You've been leading me around by the nose long enough."

Three hours later, when Maureen and I went back to our room, I described exactly how satisfying it had been to give Steve a little of his own back. A look of sheer relief came over her face.

"Thank God, Granny. I thought you'd never catch on to him. What was worse, I didn't think you'd ever realize what a terrific guy Gary is and how nuts he is about you."

"Come on, Morrie, you and I both know Gary doesn't think very highly of me. Sure, he's been great this weekend, but that's because he's stuck with me and he's making the best of it."

"Honestly, you are without a doubt the dumbest person I have ever met. Anyone with half a brain can see how he feels about you."

"Sure, he thinks I'm so great that he just has to make fun of me in front of half the student body."

"Come on, you're not still hung up about that scene at the dance, are you? Don't you realize yet that it wasn't the way you looked that made Gary crazy; it was the way you danced with Steve so long and so close. He told Toby once that you could wear a gunny sack and army boots and he'd still think you looked great."

I wasn't sure I believed a word she was saying, but it did give me something to think about. Then the next day, when Gary was delivering me to the house after dropping Maureen and Toby off, he asked me to go to a photography exhibit with him.

"It's at the art gallery next Tuesday. Since

that's the day we have to have our entries in for the photography contest, it seems an appropriate thing to do."

I'd almost forgotten about the contest. My six photos had been ready for ages. I knew they were outstanding, and I thought they had a pretty good chance of winning.

"Your father showed me your entries, Granny, and I've got to admit they're better than mine. You're sure to be the rep from our school, and if I know anything about photography, you'll win for the city and probably take the national title. You deserve it too. Your father's told me how hard you've worked to get as good as you are."

I didn't know what to say. I muttered something about being delighted to go to the exhibit with him, hoping he would get off the subject of the contest. But he didn't. Instead he started to laugh.

"I'll never forget that first day when you came into the office with the roll of film you'd taken of the football team and you didn't even know how to open the camera. I admit I was pretty angry at you at the time; I really hate cheating, as you've probably guessed. But when I realized why you'd done it and how you were really trying, I put the whole thing out of my mind. And I was right. There's nothing the least bit dishonest about you, Granny."

If he'd punched me in the stomach I couldn't

have felt any sicker. "When I realized why you'd done it." Gary was so sure I'd done it because I wanted to be a photographer, and the truth was that I'd done it just to get near Steve. Oh, no, there was nothing dishonest about Granny Tyler! Well, there was nothing I could do about the past, short of confessing and hurting him again, and what good would that do? I didn't say anything.

We ended up going to the photography exhibit together and having a terrific time. Then last Saturday he took me to a drive-in. I wasn't quite sure what to expect after my experience with Steve, but Gary, true to form, ate popcorn, drank sodas and watched the movie. I was a little hurt that he didn't try anything at all, but mostly I was just relieved. We have another date tomorrow, so we'll see what happens. I really like Gary, but I'm not sure I can ever feel about him the way I did about Steve. I guess only time will tell.

In the meantime, we've been working a lot together in the darkroom. Last night was the opening night of the play, and we worked afterwards so the prints would be ready to go to the printer today with the rest of the *Speaker* copy.

There were some wonderful shots of Maureen. Incidentally, she stole the show, just as I knew she would. The play was *Aunt Mame*, and Maureen played the title role spectacularly. The *Herald* sent a reporter to review it for the morning edition, and even he was knocked over by her talent. He did an interview with her after the show, and when Morrie told him she was going to change her name to Moonlit Forest he didn't blink an eye. That'll give you an idea how impressed he was.

Not only did Maureen give an ace performance, but she looked sensational too. She finally said farewell to her braces just before the football weekend, and the improvement was quite dramatic. She makes good photos easy to take.

There's one other shot in this edition of the *Speaker* that I'm really proud of. It's the one that goes with the article about the winner of the photography contest. I took it myself, and I caught Gary just as he heard the news — surprise and pleasure and confusion all playing across his freckles.

"I just don't understand it, Granny. Your photos of the twins were the best thing I've ever seen of little kids. How I ever beat you is a mystery to me."

And it's going to remain a mystery too. I've threatened Steve with blackmail if he ever tells Gary that I didn't enter the contest. He didn't take me seriously at first — said I didn't have anything to blackmail him with. But when I told him I'd simply make something up — just ask anyone how good I am at that — he came around.

No, I didn't do it because I felt sorry for Gary or anything else that could be considered noble. I did it for me. You see, I knew that my stuff was top quality, not because I'm so great, but because Dad showed me how to do all that wonderful stuff to my shots in the darkroom. If I'd been on my own, as Gary was, I might have won anyway. On the other hand, I might not have. The thing is, I just didn't want to get involved in any more deception.

Actually, my work wasn't a total loss. The photos I gave Judy won the girls the title of Miss Vancouver of 2000 last week. Judy's decided I walk on water and leap tall buildings, which makes life around the house pretty great. She doesn't even complain when I don't wash after I jog in the morning.

So all in all, life has turned out to be pretty good here in beautiful British Columbia. I've found a hobby that I love and that might just possibly turn out to be my career. I've got two terrific friends — Toby and Maureen. I'm dating a boy I really like and respect. I've learned that looks are not everything, and that the Steves and Lonnie Kayes of this world have problems just like everybody else; and I've got a neat family!

Oh, and there's one other thing. I bumped into this terrific looking guy yesterday — literally. He was carrying a violin case and a bunch of sheet music. Well, while we were scrambling around the floor picking up the papers, he mentioned that he was in the school's symphony orchestra.

I wonder if I should try to persuade Dad to buy me a flute.